The Prayer Place

By Tom Rattray

Dear Reader,

Although this is a work of fiction, every healing described in it is real and taken from one of the following sources:

1. My personal experience as a volunteer member of our local healing rooms.

2. Reports or observations of one of my colleagues from the healing rooms.

3. Speakers I trust whom I have personally heard at various Christian conferences.

4. Reports in credible literature, as found in the bibliography at the end of the book.

Tom Rattray

TomRattrayAuthor@gmail.com

Chapter 1

"Bomb? You want me make bomb?" Ahmed's voice rolled out like a dog's growl. He squinted dark, hooded eyes at his nephew and stamped his cigarette in the ashtray next to his chair. "Why you want bomb? My bomb time is over." He folded his Arabic language newspaper and smashed it down next to the overflowing ashtray. "No, Kamal, I no make bomb. We in America now. No more bombs." Ahmed paused, shifted his substantial body in his chair and leaned closer. His lips barely moved above his stained teeth revealing a slight smile. "Tell me, why bomb?"

Kamal Sakkab, young, tall, and muscular, fidgeted and tried to return his uncle's penetrating gaze. "I—I don't know *Al amoo,* uncle. You still know how to make the bombs. Right?"

The old man smiled. "Oh yes, many times I build. I think ... I think my favorite was the cell phone trigger. So simple, call the right number—boom." Then he frowned, "But why you want bomb?"

"It's this new place–at the mall."

"What place?"

Kamal clenched his fists and tensed his arms. "This new place they opened this summer—right in front of my kiosk at the mall. This Christian place!" He looked up at Ahmed again. "The people go in, even with their Bibles sometimes. Then later they come out all smiles and chatter.

Many even talk about how their god has healed them." He sat up straight. "I hate it! My stomach groans, my heart races, my mind screams 'Destroy this infidel place. It is evil!' "

"The other day the cookie store girl even went in." He frowned. "I liked this girl. I thought we were friends. I didn't know, but she had a problem with her foot. I never saw it because she was always behind the counter. She wore a special shoe. She came out of The Prayer Place with no shoes at all. She almost danced. She said she was going right over to the store to buy normal shoes. How do they do that?" He searched his uncle's face for a clue. "It must be some kind of trick, or magic."

Ahmed raised his eyebrows. "Did she say what happened?"

"Yes! She said they prayed and Jesus healed her foot. It was a club foot and now it was healed. A miracle she called it."

"Look at me Uncle. I do nothing, nothing for Allah. I sit on my little stool all day long and sometimes sell a few belts a wallet or a purse or two. What is that? How does that help? What would our Imam in Gaza say about that? What about the Koran?" He wrinkled his brow. "Has Allah put me right here to destroy this place? It must be uncle." He pounded his fist into his hand. "So I need a bomb, a big bomb!"

Ahmed inhaled long and deep. "Kamal, Kamal. We in America now. Remember, we now from Morocco, not Gaza, not Palestine. We have no shame of who we are. We are proud." He wagged his finger at Kamal. "But we must be smart, careful." He picked up his cigarette and took a deep drag, held it in his lungs, and released it. "This place you speak of. What is it?"

"It's like a store, but they sell nothing. Remember, when you first got me my kiosk there was a tax return place in front? That closed, and after a little while these young people brought in some tables and chairs, put up posters, and a sign. They call it The Prayer Place. I don't know what's inside.

They play their music in there. It is only open a few afternoons and Friday evening.

"Kamal, your father die when he make bomb. I not lose you too. Besides, you do not think about this right."

"What do you mean?" Kamal arched a thick brow.

"Your problem is not this place. Places are easy in America."

He looked more confused. "Okay, what is my problem?"

Ahmed smiled at him. "It's the people.

Chapter 2

The Previous April

"Marina! Paul's on the phone. Pick up the extension."

"Hi, Son."

"Hi Mom, how are you?

"I'm fine. We're both fine. Are you okay?"

"Well, that's why I'm calling. I have some exciting news. I want to bring Christ to the marketplace."

"Wow!" Frank said.

"Oh my," His mother said.

"And you believe you know how to do that, Son?"

"Yep," Paul said in measured tones. "I think I do, at least part of it, but I'm going to need your help."

"Our help?" both parents chorused. "What on earth for?"

"Well Mom, it's a little complicated. I was going to try to explain it all on the phone, but I think I'd rather do it in person."

"Great. Do you want us to come down there?"

"No, Dad. I thought we'd come to you–for the weekend, if that's alright. It's only a couple of hours drive."

"We?"

"Oh yeah, my friend, Cal, and me. You remember him, Cal Bennett? You remember, tall, blond, freckles?"

"Oh yes, a very nice boy. He can come to church with us on Sunday."

"'Man, Mother." Dad said. "Remember, they're over 21."

Paul enjoyed his parents' repartee. "Whatever. Yeah, Cal is working with me on this. Maybe he could stay in my brother's old room? I realize it's kind of short notice, but I need to fish or cut bait on this project."

"We'll be ready," Mom said. "I'm looking forward to it. Sure you don't want to come for dinner?"

"No thanks. We'll grab something here."

"I can do something simple, like sloppy joes."

Once a feeder, always a feeder. "Okay Mom. That would be great. I don't want to put you to a lot of work."

"Oh, phooey. It's my pleasure."

***

As the four of them sat around the kitchen table that Friday evening, Frank looked proudly at his son's lanky frame, chiseled chin, and tousled auburn hair. But he could stand it no longer. "Okay, son, enough chit-chat. I'm so glad you guys agreed to a meal with us. It's always a good way to start a new project. So, what's the deal? How can we help you bring Christ to the marketplace?"

Paul flashed his affable grin, glanced at Cal, and said, "Well, I need to finish my Masters of Divinity with a thesis project. I've been thinking about how to bring the lost to the Lord for a long time. Yeah, lots of other people have, too. But mostly I believe they want to get people saved and into a church. There's nothing wrong with that, of course, but that's a real stretch for lots of people."

He looked at both his parents smiling. "So, what did Christ do? He went out and talked to people and prayed for them."

Frank looked impatient. "Son, so far, this is background. What are you setting the stage for?"

Paul looked at him, pursed his lips, and said, "Okay, the big idea is that Cal and I, and a team we'll bring, will pray for people—in the mall."

Both his parents sat up. Frank raised an eyebrow. Smiling, he said, "You're not only talking about strolling down the mall to ask random people if they would like some prayer, are you?"

Paul and Cal both grinned. "Nope." Paul looked at Cal. "I told you he was a quick study."

"You want to use Mother's place." He noted them nodding. "This is just for the summer–right?"

"Yessir, we need to finish this part before the fall semester."

Cal looked confused, "Mother's place?"

Paul started to answer, but Frank interrupted. "Yes, Marina is planning to open a quilting store in the fall. I learned that a tax preparation store in the mall recently closed. So I cut a deal to hold the space for her. It's in a great location, and will be an easy conversion. Right now it's sitting there, empty. Her equipment and supplies won't come in until the fall." He thought a minute. "Naturally you haven't said what you have in mind, but it might not take much modification."

The room was silent for a moment. Paul asked, "What do you think, Dad?"

Frank smiled at his son. "I think I need to know a bit more about what you want to do. For instance, do you have a name?"

Paul nodded, "We do. We'll call it 'The Prayer Place.'"

Frank rubbed his hands together. "Good name! I like it. And what will happen in this Prayer Place?"

"Basically, people will come in and we'll pray for them. Pretty much whatever they want." Frank was silent, so Paul continued. "My thesis is that the Holy Spirit will come and take over. Like in the book of Acts. And if they're not Christians, we will give them the Gospel."

Marina exclaimed, "Oh, Paul, this is so exciting! I can't wait to see it start."

"Hold on, Mother," Frank said, as he put his hand on her arm. "There's more to this."

Paul and Cal both frowned.

"Think about it guys. You have no idea who might walk in the door. There are a lot of kooks and weirdos out there. And not everyone will think this a good idea, a good thing to be doing in a mall. And you realize that the Evil One certainly doesn't want the Holy Spirit to show up the way you expect. I'm not saying it's a bad idea, but it won't be a simple down-hill slide."

"Hm." Paul said, "Dad, I hadn't considered that." He glanced at Cal. "You agree, Cal?"

"For sure. Christ met a lot of opposition. No reason to assume we won't."

Paul looked at his dad. "Are you saying we should do something else?"

"No, I'm not saying that. Not at all. In fact, it's a terrific idea." He steepled his fingers together and held them to his lips. Then he looked Paul in the eye. "I tell you what I'd like to do. Tomorrow morning I'll call my lawyer and see what the legal ramifications are, and also the mall manager. If those are both at least yellow lights, then why don't we go look at the place in the afternoon?

Paul and Cal high-fived. "Yes!"

***

Later that evening, Paul's parents sat alone in their bedroom. His mother beamed, but Frank looked concerned. "What's the matter honey?" she asked. "Don't you think Paul's idea is exciting?"

"Exciting? Yes, yes I do. Very."

"But?"

"I sure hope they know what they are doing. Paul's a pioneer here you know."

"Yes he is. But what's the concern?"

Frank looked at her lovingly. "Most pioneers die young."

Chapter 3

Paul Shepard started to straddle his chair backwards, reconsidered, and dropped his lanky frame on the seat. A subtle smile broke through his chiseled chin as he scanned their new facility at the mall . He spoke with more authority than usual. "Gather round, folks, if you will."

Cal and Jaslyn brought their chairs into a circle. Paul said, "Mary, although you're not on the prayer team, you're very much part of this project, so you too." Mary smiled shyly, and brought her chair out from behind the folding table that had been her work station.

Cal asked, "What's up?"

Paul smiled at him, enjoying his eagerness and open approach. Caleb 'Cal' Bennett was Paul's best friend since they were undergrads at Branham. He was delighted that Cal agreed to join his summer project. "A couple of things. First, let us join in prayer to thank the Lord for giving us an excellent first week in The Prayer Place–at least it was for me."

"Amen!" Cal exclaimed as the two ladies nodded in agreement.

They were all silent for a few moments, eyes shut, deep in contemplation. Then, one by one, they spontaneously poured out their gratitude and pleasure at how much they'd been blessed.

"Thank you —and thank you, Jesus." Paul said. "Before we bail out of here, could we take a few minutes to compare notes and debrief." It was 8 PM Saturday night, and they had all been in prayer for mall walk-ins from three to eight for four days.

"Could we each give a few words about where you are right now? Jas?"

Jaslyn Malka, the 22-year-old daughter of an Ethiopian Coptic mother and Israeli father, looked at each of them. Her dark eyes glistened as a tear ran down her golden brown cheek. "Amazed, absolutely amazed. When I heard of your project and asked to join, I had no idea it'd be like this."

"Thanks, Jas. Cal?"

Cal grinned. His clear blue eyes gleamed, and he pushed back his mop of blond hair. "I'm bushed. This is hard work!" He paused, then added, "And hungry!" To chuckles and nods from the others.

Paul added, "Got it, Cal. I'd say you speak for all of us. Myself—I am humbled, humbled at how the Lord has opened so many doors —getting this place from my dad for the summer, it's almost perfect. You guys coming on board, the housing working out, and how He has permitted us to minister to total strangers —again and again."

Paul looked up, "Mary, anything to add?"

A big smile broke through her usually serious, round face. As quickly, it disappeared. "I ... I had no idea what to expect. Who'd come in, how you'd pray, what would happen? It's been like sitting in an improv theater that never ends. It's exciting! I'm honored to be even a small part of it."

"Interesting insight, Mary. Thanks." Paul paused and looked at them one by one. "Last question. What was the highlight and the lowlight of the week for you?"

Jas and Cal chorused, "Dolly's foot." Cal said, "When she came in with her cane and her foot bent over I thought, 'Oh man, why this Lord? It's too hard.' Hah! She only wanted relief from her pain. But then Paul, when you put your hand on her ankle, it just straightened out—right in front of us. That's incredible. I cried."

"We all cried, Cal. Yep, that was major. And the lowlight?"

Jas intoned. "For me, it was that old lady, that sad, lonely old lady–Portia, I recall her name was. I didn't know how to pray for her, and I didn't see that we helped her much."

"You never know, Jas. Mysterious ways–remember?" He shifted to Cal. "Cal?"

"Yeah, she was a tough one. But for me the worst was the GI with PTSD looking for work. He needed an employment counselor, not us."

"Yeah" Paul smiled. "For me, it was the ones who didn't come in. You could see them peer through the glass, sometimes more than once, and then move on. I'd love to give them enough hope to take a chance on God."

As they nodded and started to get up from their chairs, Mary spoke up, "May I make a suggestion?"

"Sure." Paul looked at her with interest.

"Well, while you were praying for people, or they were waiting their turn, I thought it would be nice to have some music playing. You know, to kind of set the mood."

"That's a great idea, Mary, soft worship music. I love it!" Paul grinned. "And I have a couple of CDs that will be perfect. I'll bring in a boom box, and maybe later we can get a real sound system."

This time, as they stood to go home, Jas muttered under her breath, "I wonder who made him king?"

Chapter 4

Vestal Hartwig sauntered along the mall and enjoyed people's reactions. The men were fun. They smiled, maybe even spoke, or whipped around in a double take. As a pure albino she only used eyeliner beneath her pale blue eyes, with a hint of lipstick. It gave her an exotic look, enhanced by her high cheekbones, narrow nose and chin, and tall, slender stature. Although she had never modeled, she emulated how they walked, and liked to see her reflection in the store windows.

Teenage boys were no longer a threat. Although they liked her long, white hair, and alabaster skin, most of them wanted access to her body. Now, at thirty-three, acceptance was no longer an issue. She was enmeshed in an adult group that welcomed and respected her.

Today's visit to the mall was uncommon, but she just felt like getting out. Perhaps she'd try to find some shoes. Her 7.5 AA foot was always a challenge, and Internet orders were seldom satisfactory. She passed a cookie place, paused, and decided against it. Why do something she'd want to undo later? Up ahead she read an unusual sign over a glass-front store. "The Prayer Place." Curious, she crossed over to view it, but had trouble seeing through the smoked glass. A middle-aged couple came out empty handed. They seemed delighted with their visit as they chattered and grinned. What did they sell in there?

For some reason she didn't want to go into the store to investigate. But the dark, attractive young man at the leather goods kiosk right in front might be familiar with it. He turned and flashed a broad smile. "Yes, my lovely lady, how may I help you today? Perhaps a fine new purse of Moroccan leather, or a beautiful beaded belt for your wardrobe?"

She blushed. "Yes, possibly. But," she pointed to The Prayer Place, "well ... well I was curious about this store here."

He frowned. "Oh, I see." He paused, "It's new."

"I thought so. What do you know about it? What do they do there?"

He paused again, and appeared to think about how he would respond, perhaps even if he should respond. "I don't know much. I guess they pray for people. The lady from the cookie store had a bad foot, and when she came out, it was all fixed. She didn't have to wear special shoes anymore."

"That's remarkable. I assume this is a Christian place?"

"Yes, I'm sure it is," he said in an almost mechanical voice.

"Hm, you don't sound very enthusiastic about it."

He smiled, "You see I'm not a Christian. So, no."

She smiled in return, "That's okay, neither am I." She looked at again., "Is it very popular? Do a lot of people go there?"

"Yeah, pretty much. They're not open a lot, but when they are, more people come lately."

"Do they charge? Do people have to pay for it?"

He shook his head. "I'm not sure, but for some reason I don't think so. Interesting question." He pursed his lips. "I wonder why they do it. And I wonder how they do it–who pays?" He looked at her, "You know, for the workers, the rent, the electricity. Somebody has to pay."

"Yes, I suppose they do." She turned to his kiosk. "But enough of that. You mentioned a beaded belt?"

A few minutes later she strode down the mall toward her car, sporting a new belt. *The coven has to hear about this.*

Chapter 5

Jaslyn looked up as Mary opened the door for a new client. The woman seemed to be trying to put on a happy face, but with a hint of tears threatening. Jas gravitated toward her right away. "Hi, I'm Jas," she said in a gentle voice, "and this is Paul and Cal. And you are?"

"Wanda, Wanda Kohler." She paused. "I didn't know you were open on Monday, but I'm so glad you are. I just took a chance." Her cloudy brown eyes searched Jas's face. She wore dark slacks and a somber print blouse. Her short brown hair was brushed back behind a headband.

"Yes, we switched to Monday, Wednesday, Friday, and Saturday, to give us some time to rest and pray in between." Jas studied her. "Would you like to sit down Wanda?" Jas queried as she eased her to a chair. "What's going on?"

"Thanks." The woman took a deep breath, pursed her lips, and looked at each of them. "I don't know what to do, where to turn. My marriage is falling apart."

Jas glanced at Paul, who frowned out of Wanda's sight. Then she leaned close to Wanda, "Can you tell us about it?"

"I don't know what's wrong. I don't think he loves me any more. He complains that nothing I do is right. 'The toast isn't buttered right. The bacon has soft spots. His shirts get wrinkled when I don't put them in the drawer right.' Any more I feel like his maid, or his servant. I used to be excited when he came home from work. Now I dread it."

She twisted and untwisted her purse strap as she continued. "I thought we'd have some kids. But no, he doesn't like kids, at least not babies. He has a kid from his first marriage that he never sees. I don't think he even cares about her.

"To be honest, I'm tired of it. I am not a bad person. I think maybe I want out." She sagged over to Jas, tears streaming down her cheeks, her nose running.

Jas pulled her chair closer and gave her a shoulder hug. "I see."

Cal offered her a wad of tissues. "Thanks. Fritz never gives me anything."

"So, what was it like in the beginning?" Jas asked.

Wanda looked up at Jas, wiping her tears away. "At first it was okay, actually good. We used to do things together. You know, go bowling, maybe a movie. He took me camping a couple of times. He likes to shoot, so I would go to the range with him, although it wasn't my thing. But over time he started to complain that I wasn't any fun, and he'd rather hang out with his buddies from the plant."

She paused again, overcome with emotion. Between sobs she choked out, "At night now he says I'm not sexy enough. I don't dress like he wants." Her shoulders shook and she bent almost double in grief. "We haven't been intimate in months, and when we are I feel like he's almost raping me. There's no tenderness, no," she searched for a word, "no love."

"I'm scared. I thought I was a good wife. I try to please him." She looked at Jas, "What should I do?"

Jas was bewildered. She looked up at Paul for help. He knelt next to Wanda, and put his hand gently on her shoulder. "Wanda, I need to ask you something."

She wiped her red eyes, and looked at him.

"How much of what you've been telling us have you told him?"

She reared back, held her hands up, eyes wide open. "I can't. He hates to talk about us."

"Does he ever hit you?"

"No, but he throws things, smashes them. It's real scary."

Paul stood up, took a step back, and looked at Wanda. "You're at the end of your rope aren't you?"

She nodded and sobbed again. Jas hugged her tight.

Paul asked, "Where is your husband right now?"

Barely audible, she choked out, "He's right outside, in the waiting room, but I can't ... I can't tell him any of his."

"Does he have any idea why you're here?"

She shrugged. "I dunno. I was real vague about why I wanted to come."

"Wanda, do you mind if I have a short conversation with my prayer partners for a moment? Will you be okay in here?"

"Yeah, I guess so. Sure."

**

Paul signaled Jas and Cal to come to the next consultation room with him. "This is not a primary prayer need. They need marriage counseling, heavy duty. I'm going to talk to her husband. If he seems amenable to it, I will suggest they get some help. I'll get a recommendation from church by Wednesday. Can I ask you two to pray with her for strength and guidance while I talk to her husband?"

They both agreed immediately.

"Great. By the way Jas, I thought you were very good with her. Real heart."

Jas grinned. "Thanks, boss. Sorry about my smart comment Saturday evening. I was tired and not thinking. You can be my king—in here."

They all chuckled.

***

Paul stepped into the waiting area, only one man there. He had male pattern balding, with close cropped hair. His black tee shirt accentuated his bulging biceps and full midsection. He looked up.

"Are you Fritz?"

Fritz squinted, "Yeah. Who are you?"

"I'm Paul, the Director here. How are you doing?"

"Hey man, I'm, doing fine, just fine," he said in a firm, hard voice. "What did my wife tell you?"

"Well, Fritz, everything our clients tell us is confidential, to protect them. But I need to ask you something."

"Okay," Fritz folded his arms and leaned back. "What?"

"Do you love your wife?"

Fritz looked up at Paul, frowned, and said nothing. Then he seemed to think about it, and nodded his head. "Yeah, I guess. Yeah, I do, I love her." He paused, "maybe haven't been doing a real good job of late.

"Well Fritz, my colleagues are praying for God's wisdom for Wanda right now. This is not my area, but I strongly believe that you two would benefit a lot from some good marriage counseling."

"She tell you that?"

"No, Fritz, she didn't. This is my conclusion." I'd like to ask some trusted friends of mine to give me a recommendation of a good counselor, and have it by Wednesday. Is that okay with you?"

Fritz seemed to relax, and stood up. "Okay, man. I'll give it a shot.' He reached out to shake Paul's hand. "Thanks, buddy."

He noticed Wanda enter the waiting room with Jaslyn and Cal right behind. "Ready, honey?" he smiled.

She looked surprised, "Yes, dear,"

He held the door open for her as they went back in the mall.

****

The team watched in pleasant surprise. Paul said, "Thank you, Jesus."

Chapter 6

Eddie French groaned as he tried to roll out of bed. As usual, his back felt like someone had used a baseball bat on it during the night. The Vicodin he'd finally taken at 1:00 AM had worn off. He hated to take it because it was so addictive, but he had to sleep. It was about the only thing that worked for him anymore.

At least he had stopped wasting his time with a chiropractor. That was the good news. The bad news was that he stayed with the guy far too long until Doctor Majoros discovered prostate cancer. Now it was in his kidneys and established in his pancreas. And he felt like he'd been dragged down a railroad track.

He pushed himself to sit up and cradled his head in his hands. How would he get himself to the doctor this morning? He took a deep breath and let it out. Sitting up was better than on his back. "Oh man," he moaned, "Come on Eddie, you can do this."

He clutched the night-stand and slowly rose to his feet and grabbed the headboard to stop swaying. He gagged and quick shuffled into the bathroom, bent over the toilet, and heaved up most of the little supper he had last night. At last the heaves subsided, but the nausea never did.

He gripped the vanity and stepped in front of the sink. He popped all nine of his morning meds into his mouth and took a big swig of water. He swirled them around and gulped them down in one swallow. A couple more sips but no more. Although he was supposed to take a lot of liquid, water was a chancy prospect, especially in the morning. Maybe some herbal tea in a few minutes. That seemed to work better.

He ran his brush through the few tufts of hair still left and dabbed on some deodorant. At least he almost never needed to shave anymore. Anyway, he'd quit messing with his appearance. People would do a double take when they saw him and then look away. He didn't blame them. His hollow red eyes, sallow skin, and baggy cheeks could've come from a Hollywood make-up room.

Time to try for breakfast? A slice of toast, some apple juice, and a cup of Echinacea Plus tea with a little honey usually stayed down. Eggs—and bacon were from the distant past. He wasn't up to cooking anyway. His last pancake was ancient history, and he used to love them.

Forty-three minutes later he pulled his Honda Accord into the last available handicapped space at the Doctor's complex. Thank goodness it was a short, easy drive. His days to break speed records were long gone, and today he was happy just to make it.

A few minutes later the nurse took his vitals and discovered he had a mild fever. At least he hadn't needed to sit in the waiting room with all the other cancer patients. Most of them looked sallow and frail, like him.

Dr. Majoros listened to his heart and lungs. "Eddie, how are you?"

"Not good, doc, I feel like crap. But you tell me, you're the doc."

The doctor cleared his throat and pulled up his stool. "Eddie, I know this is a rough time for you, and I am so sorry. I'd hoped we'd be able to get on top of this by now and make you a lot more comfortable. But I've looked at your latest scans and labs, and the Gemcitabine plus Tarceva haven't been as effective as I'd hoped. So we need to help boost your immune system and turn this around."

"Sounds right Doc. Can you tell me what stage you would call it now?"

The doctor pursed his lips and frowned. He looked Eddie in the eye. "At this stage, Eddie, I'd call it stage four. What that means is that the cancer has spread from the original site, in your case your prostate gland, to an accompanying gland–the kidneys. However, it has now done what we call distant spread, when it moves to other, unrelated organs–your pancreas. That makes it stage four." He put his hand on Eddie's shoulder. "I know this sounds bad, but believe me, we have more options. We have ruled out surgery, but I'm thinking that Degarelix would be good for you. Are you okay with that?"

Eddie shrugged and looked at the doctor with tear-filled eyes. "Doc, at this point I'm ready to try anything. Sure, you're the expert, not me. If this new one is better, let's do it."

"It's possible to still lick this. I've seen it before." He stood. "You sit tight for a minute, and we'll phone in the new scrip."

Back in his car Eddie sat. He shook his head and hung it low. "This will not end well, I know it. But," he looked up, started the engine, and checked his mirrors, "I need to keep positive." He eased his car out to the street and drove to the mall to get his new medication. Activity was always therapeutic.

After the stop at the pharmacy, Eddie capitulated to his ever narrowing waist. He'd cinched up his baggy pants and punched new holes in his belt for the last time. So today called for a couple pairs of slimmer pants at the department store. On the way out he spotted the cookie place and a leather goods kiosk beyond. A cookie and a nice new belt might cheer him up.

As he picked through the belts, he saw a new store, The Prayer Place. He always regarded himself as an agnostic and never went to church. But for some reason his Grandmother Wilson came to mind, and one of her favorite quotes, "Despise not the day of small beginnings."–from the Bible he guessed. She had very strong faith and did her best to get him to adopt it.

What the heck. He pushed through the glass door and stepped up to the desk. A young lady smiled at him, not put off by his ghastly appearance. "Hi, I'm Mary. Would you like prayer?"

"Whoa, there." He held up his hand. "I'm only curious. What is it you do here? What do you sell?"

"Oh, we don't sell anything. We love to pray for people. We're students from Branham Seminary down in Kentucky, here for the summer, and we'd love to pray for you if you like."

Eddie smiled for the first time in weeks. "I'm sure you would. So what happens when you pray?"

"Oh, that's up to God, of course. Many times people get better, get what they ask God for."

Eddie raised his eyebrows, "Really? Tell me, have you ever prayed for cancer?"

Mary frowned, "I don't think so, not yet. This is only our second week, but we'd love to pray to heal cancer." She paused and looked him in the eye.

He returned her look. "And what do you charge for this service?"

"Oh, there's no charge. God's love is free, to everyone. So are we."

"Okay, thanks,." Eddie said and backed out through the door to the mall.

Strange, very strange. I actually liked being in there.

Chapter 7

Mary filed her papers in a cardboard box. "I wonder where I can get a desk," she muttered to herself.

"I heard that." Paul said as he came up next to her.

"Oh! I didn't see you." She looked at him and smiled. "You must be tired. It's been super busy the last few days."

"It sure has. And yep, I am tired. As much as I love this work, it's more than I bargained for." He took a deep breath and sank into a chair.

"I can see that. I wish I could help more." She looked into his eyes.

Paul rested his hand on her arm. "Mary, you've been a lifesaver. As you may have noticed, organization is not my strong suit. We'd be in total chaos if it weren't for you. The change to Monday Wednesday, Friday and then Saturday is much better. And the sign-in clipboard and the client information sheets you did were brilliant. We couldn't do this without you."

She dared to put her hand on his, for the first time. "Thanks, Paul. We had to do something. Today they were lined up outside the door when I got here." She paused and bit her lip. "Paul, I have to tell you this. You need to get help. Get more people to pray. The clients come back for repeat visits, and the word is out. God is working here–big time, and the healings don't stop.

"For instance, that lady today, Kathy somebody. When she came in, she looked like she wore a back brace or something. Only she wasn't. I don't know what you did, but when she came out of the prayer room, she almost danced. Paul, you have a gift, a real gift at work here."

Paul grinned. "Yeah, she was pretty cool. When she talked about her neck and shoulders and spine, I got a picture of a heavy weight, like a concrete yoke or backpack, on her. It prompted me to ask her about her family and she teared up. Turns out she takes care of two elderly parents and an adult brother. He's into heroin. And she has a husband, two kids, and her own job. Nobody could do that, especially alone."

Paul's eyes glistened. "It was a spiritual burden. When I prayed to lift it off and give her cares to Jesus, it was like a weight came off her. She stood taller and twisted her neck all around. She said she couldn't do that for years. Yeah, it was really cool." His eyes glistened.

"That's my point. You have a gift. Cal and Jas do too. Kathy was only one healing. Remember the man deaf in one ear? How about the boy whose head shook all the time? And the fixed knees? We should have run a special on knees this week.

"But you need help." She squeezed his hand. "You'll wear yourself out. Even Jesus went into the desert for restoration–multiple times. Let me help you. I'd like to speak to Pastor Andy, get a few ideas from him. Is that okay?

Paul answered slowly, "Yes, I guess so. But, gee—new people? Strangers? It would be, ah—different." He stopped, appeared to be in deep thought. "But you're right. We need help." He grabbed her by the shoulders. "Okay, Mary Poppins! You're on. You are the spoonful of sugar that makes the medicine go down. Go for it. Tell me what I can do to help." He gave her a shoulder hug.

Mary smiled. *He has no idea how I feel about him.*

Chapter 8

Kamal pulled into the Islamic Center. He'd tried similar groups at nearby universities and found this was the best place to meet guys with similar beliefs. Most of the rest were social clubs, with little or no allegiance to Sharia law. Here he found a few North African expatriates like himself who wanted to promote Islam.

The Center was an older house fixed up as a meeting place, and a small mosque with a copper-colored dome atop a two story glassed in tower next to the entrance. Kamal parked to the left of the house, and stepped into the cool, with subdued lights and a sweet aroma escaping from the kitchen. The afternoon sun produced a placid, serene atmosphere.

A young man called out, "Kamal! How are you doing?"

"Hey Yasir, doing great! How are you?" Yasir was the man he'd hoped to meet. "Got time for some tea?"

"For you, of course."

Kamal clapped him on the shoulder as they ambled to the samovar for tea. "Let's find a quiet place to talk."

Yasir looked askance at Kamal. "Sounds serious. You got something on your mind?"

"I do." He ushered them both to a corner in a small side room. They squatted cross-legged on low mats and placed their tea on a low table. Kamal took a sip of tea. "You said you came from Libya as I recall. That must have been in Qadaffi's time – right?" Yasir nodded.

"Correct. We left soon after his death in '11. My dad planned to come here for some time. He said he was tired of all the conflict."

"We did similar things in Morocco. Ah, can I ask, did your dad join the Brotherhood?"

Again Yasir looked at him cautiously. "Why do you ask?"

Kamal smiled. "I hoped it might be something we have in common. I was Brotherhood in Palestine, and then Morocco—below the radar."

Yasir looked startled. "I didn't know you were Palestinian. Wow, that's a surprise."

Kamal smiled again, a bit embarrassed. He held his hand out, calm down. "Shh. I tell no one about that, other than family. You're the first one. Yeah, I was Brotherhood trained as a kid. The whole family was. Well, not my mom or my sister, but my brothers and my dad and me. "

Yasir sat back, his eyes wide open, eyebrows raised. "Man, that's amazing. Praise Allah! So was I." He paused, then leaned close and whispered, "Did you do any missions?"

Kamal nodded. "A few. Most times I was a look-out or a messenger. I just started the good action when we went to Casablanca. That was all about politics, elections–that kind of stuff. How about you?"

Yasir clasped Kamal's forearm. "I had no idea. This is so great. I was pretty young then. But I spent a month at a desert camp. Naturally we had a lot of Koran, but we learned basic small arms, RPGs, smuggling, surveillance, how to communicate – oh yeah, and a lot of physical conditioning. And I mean a lot."

"Bombs?"

Yasir shook his head. "No. That was advanced, not for kids." Once again he looked at Kamal. "My friend, what are you thinking about? What's going on?"

Kamal sipped his tea and did not answer right away. "Have you ever been to my stand in the mall? I don't recall that you have."

"No, never seen it. You want to show it to me? You want to burn it down for the insurance money?" Yasir grinned.

Kamal glanced at his watch. "Not exactly. You got time to see it now? I want to show you what I have in mind, not only talk about it."

"Sure I guess so. Why don't I follow you? I live out that way and can go home afterwards."

"You're on."

Half an hour later they stood in front of Kamal's leather goods stand. His assistant knew to give them some space and went out for a smoke. Kamal put his hand on Yasir's shoulder and walked him around the end of the stand. He whispered in his ear. "Don't point, but I want you to look at the store in front of us."

"The Prayer Place? What about it? I never heard of it. What do they sell?"

"That's it. They sell nothing. They pray for people, sick people."

"And do they get well?"

"Yes!" Kamal hissed. "Again and again."

"Are you serious? Unbelievable. Is it a church?"

"I don't think so. I think it's a few college kids who do this. It boils my blood. I hate it. If it was a church in their own building I wouldn't mind, but right here, in the mall, and in front of my stand day after day. It isn't right."

"There seem to be a lot of people inside."

"More and more, every day they are here. They even line up at the door to wait for it to open."

Yasir studied Kamal. "So what do you want to do? Why am I here?"

"I want your help. You're an engineer, right?"

"Yes." He said in a very measured voice. "Help with what?"

"Make it go away."

"How?"

Kamal raised both hands. "Boom."

Yasir's eyes were as big as saucers. "You want to blow it up?"

Kamal nodded, "I want to try. I can't stand it." He paused a studied his friend. "Do you want to help?"

Yasir took a deep breath and let it out. Then he returned Kamal's steady gaze. "Okay."

Chapter 9

Pastor Andy Oates looked around the circle and smiled. Relaxed in jeans and a tee, bushy-haired with a trim goatee, his smile put everyone at ease. He always enjoyed the regular Thursday night prayer meeting. Many of his most ardent members attended every week, and the prayer was rich and powerful. He always felt God's presence in the room. "Evening folks. Everyone doing okay?" He studied their faces and waited for the needs to show up as they always did.

"Marina, have you got something on your mind?"

A middle-aged woman brushed her hair back from her face. "Very perceptive, pastor. Are you familiar with the place my son has started in the mall, The Prayer Place?"

"Yes. I saw it the other evening. It was closed, but I must admit I was curious. This must be what you mentioned a few days ago. Can you tell us what it is?"

She looked very proud. "Yes. It's a free prayer service for anyone who wants it. Paul and his friends from seminary are here for the summer. Their project is taking Christ to the marketplace. It's doing well, almost too well."

Andy frowned, "How can that be?"

"It's booming. There's only three of them that pray, and an office girl. Paul comes home exhausted and often seems burdened. He said they have to turn people away. They've had a lot of healings, some of them quite remarkable. The word is out and more people want to come. They've added hours to be open, but only have so much energy, even for young people."

"Well I understand that, Marina. Scripture says, 'The effective fervent prayer of a righteous man avails much.' What it doesn't say is that it's also tiring. This would be more so than some intercession. Since they pray for total strangers they have to be alert to understand and discern their needs as well as pray." He paused and grinned at Marina. "But what a wonderful problem to have. Let's look at Jesus for guidance. What did he do? Anybody?"

A white-haired man raised his hand. "He rested, took breaks, went into the wilderness, rowed across the lake to get away from people. It doesn't say so, but I bet he took naps too. I sure do."

Andy chuckled, "Great, Sam, so do I. And what else did he do folks?" A few people fidgeted, looked at each other, but remained silent. "He recruited, got a team of twelve, not three." He looked at Marina. "I love your mother's heart, Marina. Paul's a lucky boy, but he's in deeper than he expected. It's time to shift from prayer warrior to prayer manager, at least in part."

He looked around. "Most of you are on our healing team at the Sunday service. How about it folks, who could help?" Everyone raised their hand. He turned to Marina, "What do you think, Mom? Would he mind a little help from the church?"

Marina gasped as tears flooded her eyes, "Oh yes, that would be wonderful. Oh my, pastor, I didn't come tonight to ask you to become part of this."

"I know you didn't. God did."

Chapter 10

Vestal eased her little Honda into a slot near the barn. This remote location was perfect for a coven to meet, and her favorite. A lot of the girls loved nature, and walked in the nearby woods before they met. They used a fire ring out back that she'd come to when the meetings were in early spring or late fall, out of bug season. Since today's forecast was rain, they were inside.

She lifted the latch on the barn door, stepped over the transom, took a deep breath and smiled. Candle fragrance and incense swept over her. Most of the women sat in a circle on mats in front of candles or satanic symbols or objects. The altar on the left was draped to cover most of the blood drips on the legs and floor. Several of her friends looked up and smiled. Sybil stood and came over to hug her. "Vestal Hartwig, as I live and breath. How are you? I haven't seen you in months."

"I'm fine, Sybil, it's so good to see you." Vestal stepped back to study her friend. Sybil was short, a little chunky, and dressed in a black, filmy sheath. Her long black hair hung over her shoulders, framing a tapered pale face with dark eyes and several studs and rings on her nose, lips and ears. "I hoped you'd be here. I have news and a project idea."

Allegra McKivven, a thin, older woman stood up. Since it was her family's barn she was the informal hostess. "Ladies, I think we're all here. There's tea, juice or wine on the shearing table. Help yourself. Don't mind the noise of the goats in the back. We might offer one up later. Vestal, it's good to see you. Do you have something you want us to hear?"

"Thanks Allegra. Yes, I do. Let me first say it's so good to back in The Gathering. I'm sorry to miss the last few meetings, but I don't do outdoors insects very well." She looked around at the uplifted faces.

"Okay, have any of you been to the Colony Mall in the last few weeks?" Nobody responded. "I'm not surprised. I almost never go there myself. But I was there a few days ago and there's a new place, they call The Prayer Place. It's not quit a store. I didn't go into it, but the leather goods guy in front says people go there for prayer, and often get healed of various things. He says it's real popular—and free." She nodded her head. "That's right, it's kind of like a walk-in church, I guess. Anyway, I find this very objectionable. Churches belong in their own place, not in the mall."

Several women voiced assent.

"So, I wondered if any of you would be interested in working with me to shut it down, put them out of business?" Once again, she looked at the ladies, pleased to see several smiles.

"How would we do that?" Mollie was a newer member, young, short and chubby, with an open, innocent face and bobbed hair.

Vestal smiled, "Mollie, it's Mollie—right? I'm not sure. That's the project. I know other covens have done similar things and sabotaged various church activities. Would you like to help me work it out? How about you Sybil?"

After Vestal got a list of volunteers to help, she sat next to Sybil. As the meeting wound down, she leaned over to her friend. "But how are you, my dear?" Vestal looked at her again and noted an unexpected swelling. "Are you, ah ...?"

"Expecting, yes, very observant. Was it planned? No, I wouldn't say so. In fact, not at all."

"Oh," Vestal paused to think. "Have you decided what you ... you know?"

"What I'll do with the baby?" Sybil almost whispered. "It's a big decision. The first time was so special, so enriching when we offered up that little life to Molech. I will never forget it, never be the same."

"What about the father?"

"Hah! That jerk? I didn't want his genes in my kid anyway, but he's no longer with us."

You threw him out?"

"Well, sort of. When I say he's no longer with us, I mean he is no longer with us—or anyone. He's gone, kaput, finito."

Vestal's eyes opened wide. "Oh my, Sybil!"

"Shh, shh." Sybil put her finger to her lips. "Not to worry sweetie. No harm, no foul." She looked up at Vestal again. "I guess you just learned something about me."

Vestal nodded in comprehension. "Oh my, yes." She hugged Sybil again, and breathed in her ear. "You are quite a woman, quite a woman."

She smiled up at Vestal. "Thanks. And let's face it, I don't think I'm cut out to be a mother."

Chapter 11

Dr. Edwards scooted his stool over to Eddie. "Eddie, do you still work?

"Not much any more. I just can't hack it. They are very understanding, and have a primo medical plan. I tried to go in, but my boss said to stop. I wasn't doing much and he said I look so bad it upset the secretaries."

" And how old are you? Twenty-four – right?"

"Yeah, although right now I feel like I'm a hundred and twenty-four." He looked at the doctor. *Where was he going with this?*

"And you live alone as I recall. Do you have any family here?"

"Nope. I came down two years ago after school and didn't know anybody. My dad is long gone–dead. Mom lives in Akron with my only brother nearby to help her." Eddie stopped, already worn out from the trip to the office and the little bit of conversation. "Do I need to go into the hospital?"

The doctor pursed his lips. "No," he intoned and frowned. "But you need total rest and as little activity as possible—to give the medication a chance to work. Right now, you do everything right? Such as meals, food shop, laundry, manage your meds, etc."

"Yeah, I do. And it wears me out. Are you referring to a live-in nurse or something like that?"

The doctor smiled. "Normally, that's what I would say. But you aren't the usual patient. A handsome virile bachelor alone in a new town."

"Not very virile lately, Doc."

"No, I guess not at the moment. But I'm not ready to give up." The doctor paused again. "There are several possibilities. We have various services—people who come in to do meals, housework, maybe help you food shop. They don't live with you, but come in at scheduled times."

"Gee, Doc. I never thought about it. I guess that might help."

"Another possibility is that you spend time in a rehab facility until you get your strength back."

"Oh man, those places are full of old people, waiting to die. I'm not so sure about that." Eddie paused for a moment. "Doctor, let me ask you something."

The doctor looked surprised. "Sure, what is it?"

"Do you believe in prayer?"

The doctor nodded. "Yes, I do. I pray for you, you know."

Eddie smiled, "Thanks," he breathed.

"Why do you ask? What have you got in mind?"

"Well, I'm not a churchy kind of guy. Never was. We didn't go, except sometimes at Christmas once or twice. But I ran into a new place at the mall where they pray for people." He paused to gain his breath and looked at the doctor. "Do you think they might help me? Would it be a good idea to get prayed for?"

The doctor looked surprised. "Sure, it wouldn't hurt."

Eddie smiled, "Okay, I'll give it a shot."

Chapter 12

Paul slid into his chair at the kitchen table. "Hi Mom." He smiled. "Yes, I slept well."

Marina laughed. "I guess I do ask that regularly. You ready for some eggs today? Son, you have to keep your strength up. The food court is not the healthiest of places to eat all the time."

"Okay, okay. How about both eggs and some toast with your home-made blueberry jelly?"

She nodded. "Cal sleeping in today?"

"Nope, he was rolling out when I came down. He'll be here soon." Paul paused, "You know, Mom, I never really thanked you for letting him stay here this summer. It's a big help. So—thanks mom."

His mother smiled. "You're welcome son. We're happy to do it. He seems like a very nice young man."

"Yeah, he is." Paul looked up as his father came in. "Morning Dad. You doing all right?"

"Sure son, doing fine."

George Shepard was tall, with salt-and-pepper hair, deep-set blue eyes, and a craggy face. Paul always thought he looked like he a sea captain or a lumberjack. "Son, you know I continue to think about your little venture this summer. Do you have any intercessory prayer cover for it?"

Paul frowned, "Um, no, I guess not. Do you think we need it?"

George grinned. "With the healings you're getting? Absolutely. The bad guy doesn't like this one bit. And for sure some folks don't understand it, or just don't agree with it. The word is out. God is doing something powerful at the mall."

"Really? That's so cool!" Paul paused a moment. "Yeah, I see what you mean about prayer cover." He drew in a deep sigh and let it out. "Okay, something else to do."

George put his hand on Paul's shoulder. "Son, you don't have to do it all yourself. How about I talk to Pastor Oates and my men's prayer group about this?"

"Excellent! That would be great."

"Have the volunteers from church shown up yet?"

"They sure have, and they're excellent! We've even mix up the teams. School people and church people pray together for the same guest." Paul looked up with tears in his eyes. "I am totally blown away with the healings we see. It's miraculous. No other word for it, miraculous."

Paul's parents beamed.

"Wonderful, son. Thank you, Jesus." His mother said.

They all hugged as Cal stepped into the room. "Oops, didn't realize there was a love-in for breakfast."

George laughed and pulled Cal into the circle—"Not a private party, Cal. We are thankful for you too."

***

Paul and Cal slipped in the employee back door to The Prayer Place. Everyone else sat around the break table with their coffee. "Hi folks, sorry we're late." Paul looked around at them and smiled. "Before we open up, I want to mention that my parents suggested that we get some intercessory prayer cover; and it's a great idea. Does that sound right to you?"

Everyone nodded. Someone said, "For sure. Can't go into battle naked."

"Great. Okay, are we ready to roll?" Paul noticed Mary wince. "Mary?"

"Paul, I believe we need to be selective about who we accept for prayer." She paused, seemed embarrassed with everyone's attention. "You may have seen that we get several repeat people the last few days. Including ones with needs that are a bit trivial—like what clothes to wear on a date. How about we need to say they must be eighteen or with a parent?"

Jas groaned, "Oh I remember that one. Girl just couldn't make up her mind."

Julius Green, one of the new people from church, said, "That's a new one to me. But there's another area you might want to consider—counseling. We're not trained or licensed counselors. I don't know about you folks, but Cal and I got a couple and an unemployed vet yesterday who both really needed counseling, not prayer. And we couldn't help either one very much."

Mary spoke up. "Might I suggest that I pull together a set of guidelines for us, and maybe some kind of sign we can put on the window to tell what we are and what we are not?"

Paul looked around and saw unanimous agreement. "You're on, Mary, and thank you for catching this. Well done."

Mary blushed and smiled. "Thank you, Paul."

***

An older man walked into the prayer booth with his information sheet. Paul and Carla, another recent addition to the team from church, greeted him.

"Hi, I'm Paul and this is Carla. And you are?" Paul reached for the outstretched information sheet and read, "Nick Harbough. Hi, Nick." He read further. "It says here you want prayer for your fingers." Paul looked at Nick.

Nick held up his left hand. The first three fingers were minus two joints. "Lost a fight with a table saw a few years back. Stupid, mega stupid. Good thing I wasn't a harp player." He smiled.

Paul winced. "Ouch! Sure is." Paul pursed his lips and took a deep breath. "What would you like us to pray for?"

Nick's eyes teared up. "I want my fingers back. I've heard great things about this place—unbelievable things. But what the heck, no harm in trying."

"Right. Nick, tell me, are you a Christian?"

"Yeah, I guess so. I mean I don't go to church like I ought to, or read the Bible that much. Is that a problem? But I believe in God and Jesus as His son, and I pray for stuff sometimes." He looked at them.

Carla responded, "Not a problem with me. But it's not up to us. We don't heal anyone. God does. So why don't we ask Him?"

Nick closed his eyes and held out his maimed hand. Paul and Carla both took it. Paul put his other hand on Nick's head and asked the Holy Spirit to come onto him, cleanse him, fill him, and comfort him."

As he spoke, she nodded towards Nick's hand.

Paul looked surprised, "I'll get to that."

"Paul, you don't need to. Look!"

Nick's fingers were completely restored.

Chapter 13

Although Kamal's day was slow, he had to admit to himself that the increased business at The Prayer Place spilled over to his sales. Those people seem so happy and friendly. An old guy eased the door shut as he came out and grinned like he had just won the lottery. He looked up at Kamal, who smiled in response, even though he didn't want to. "You appear very pleased, sir. Would you like to celebrate with a new belt?"

The man almost danced over to him. "Yeah, good idea. But let me show you something," he said, as he reached for his cell phone.

Kamal was baffled but interested. He waited while the man thumbed his phone searching for a photo. He held it up for Kamal's inspection.

"What am I seeing, sir?" A man's hand, but with missing fingers.

"That's my hand, or it was my hand. I took this before I went in for prayer. You know, like in case something happened." He held up his hand and wiggled his fingers. "Look!" he cried, with tears in his eyes. "Jesus gave me back my fingers. It's a miracle. I still can't believe it!" He put away his phone and pulled the ends of his fingers. "They don't come off. They're real. I can feel with them—everything. Thank you, Jesus!" he cried.

Kamal said, "Well, that's wonderful for you, sir." His stomach churned. "Here, let me show you our fine selection of belts. Would you like brown or black?"

After the old man got his new belt and left, Kamal was still tense. His fists clenched, his jaw tightened, his nostrils flared. How did they do this? What was all this Jesus stuff? Why don't they know Islam is the way and the light and the only answer, and Allah is the one true God? He had to do something—and he knew what. He reached for his cell phone. "Yasir? Hi, it's Kamal. Praise be to Allah to you. Say, are you someplace where we can talk for a few minutes?"

"Yes, wait a minute," Yasir said. Kamal heard him close his office door. "Okay."

"Good. You remember that I asked if you wanted to help me with a bomb?"

Yasir said after a moment. His voice was barely audible. "Yes, how could I forget? I've thought a lot about how to do it. I figured out what we can do now. In fact, it won't be that hard."

"Excellent!" Kamal whispered and looked around since he was in the mall. "They do all kinds of things at that place. This has to stop. I want to do it as soon as possible before they become even more popular. What should I do to start?"

Yasir laughed, "My, you are eager man. Okay. I say we need to build a test unit first and detonate it in a remote place so we can see what happens, and learn how to place the real one."

Kamal said with little enthusiasm, "Yeah, I guess that's wise. See, that's why I need your help. You are so good at these things. So, can we use my garage? It's private and has an old workbench. Tell me, what do you need? What can I get?

"Okay. If you want, go to a home improvement store and buy a piece of pipe, about twelve inches long, two inches in diameter, and threaded on both ends. The kind of pipe doesn't matter as long as it's metal. No plastic. Then get two caps to thread on the ends. Can you do that?"

"Yeah, sure. I will get it on the way home. Anything else?"

"Do you have an electric drill and some drill bits?"

"Yes! I do. A good one."

"Good. Bring them. I will have the rest, gun powder, a fuse and detonation system."

"I love it! I am so excited. Praise be to Allah."

"Kamal, when do you want to do this?"

"Tonight!"

Chapter 14

Eddie got through his morning pill routine in the bathroom without once looking in the mirror. He hid the last few wisps of his hair under a knit cap, skipped shaving since he never needed to anymore. He stuffed a banana in one coat pocket, a juice bottle in the other, and shuffled out to the parking lot. If he had to heave while driving, he'd have to pull over and go on the road. Wouldn't be the first time.

Nuts! He'd forgotten that somebody was in his handicapped spot next to the door. A young kid had just unlocked the car door.

Eddie tried to raise his voice. "You realize you're in a handicap parking place? I don't see a tag."

"So—nobody really uses those," the kid replied as he opened the door. He glanced at Eddie's ashen face, stooped posture, and cane. "Oh crap. I'm sorry, man. Was this your spot?"

Eddie nodded, thankful that the kid wouldn't do it again, but he sure didn't need the reminder of how terrible he looked. "That's okay, buddy. Next time let me have it, okay?"

"For sure." The kid stood up. "Hey, can I help you— like get to your car or anything?"

"Yeah, thanks. An arm to lean on would be nice. I'm pretty shaky these days, especially in the morning. It's the blue Honda over there."

The youth approached with caution, not sure what to do. "You, ah, sick—or what?"

Eddie smiled at him. "The big C. Probably going down for the count."

"Oh man, that's rotten. What a bummer."

Eddie took his arm as they navigated their way to his car. "Yeah, not much fun. Wish me luck."

"What for? Where are you going?"

"To the mall, that Prayer Place." Eddie looked at him, "You heard of it?"

"Yeah, I have. Good luck. I'm Marty, by the way."

Eddie held out his feeble hand, "Eddie, Eddie French."

Eddie smiled as he drove away. He might have made a friend. Lousy disease was good for something.

***

Need a walker, one with a seat, Eddie thought as he approached The Prayer Place in the mall. He was exhausted. Would God show up? Nothing else ever did. He leaned against the door, but didn't have the strength to open it.

The young lady he spoke to the first time came around and opened it. "Hi! Good to see your back. For prayer this time?" She was so darned cheery.

"Yeah, I guess so. Chemo meds sure don't work—except to make me sick." He looked around, "Say, is there some place I can sit? I'm about to fall over."

"Sure, sure. Right here." She pointed to an overstuffed easy chair. "Is this okay?"

"If you don't mind, a straight chair is better. If I plop down in that, I'll never get up."

She hustled into another little room and came back with a sturdy chair. "Will this work?" She looked concerned. "I'll help you with the little form we ask people to fill out before prayer."

"That'd be great. First, let me rest a few minutes." He struggled to get his arm out of his coat sleeve, and she slid it off for him.

"I'm Mary. You take your time. Let me know when you're ready."

"Hi Mary. I'm Eddie, Eddie French. Thanks for the help." he whispered as he leaned his head back and closed his eyes. Moments later, his head slumped forward.

***

Mary tip-toed away and found Paul in a prayer cubicle. "There's somebody out here you should see. It's his first time for prayer, but he was in a few days ago to check us out."

Paul and Cal came around the corner, stopped at a distance from Eddie, took one glance, and prayed for him. Paul whispered to Mary, "What's wrong with him?"

"I'm pretty sure it's cancer. No idea what kind."

Eddie stirred and opened his eyes. "Wow," he said in a low voice, "That's never happened before." He looked up. "I've never fallen asleep sitting up. I have a hard enough time in bed." He stretched and sat up straighter. "Man, I feel better. It's so ... so peaceful here." He looked at Paul and Cal. "Are you the guys that will pray for me?"

Paul grinned. "We've already started." He held out his hand. "I'm Paul, and this is Cal, and yes, we'd love to pray for you. Can you come into a prayer room so we can have a little privacy? You can tell us what's going on."

"Sure, that's what I came for." Eddie said. "To be honest, I think this is my last option."

"Well, you're in the right place." Paul said as he and Mary helped Eddie sit comfortably for prayer.

Twenty minutes later the three men exited the cubicle. Mary looked up at Paul and gestured to ask how it went. Paul raised his eyebrows and shrugged like he wasn't sure.

Eddie shuffled toward the door. "Thanks, guys, thanks a lot. I will check my counts with my doctor and let you know. I can't say if they're any better, but I feel better. I really appreciate it."

Paul patted him on the shoulder. "You're welcome Eddie. It's what we do. No sweat if you want to come again. Lots of people do. By the way, most healings are progressive, not all at once."

Eddie looked around at him with a raised eyebrow. He pursed his lips. "Oh, okay."

***

Mary hung up the phone and signaled to Paul. "That was Eddie French—from a couple days ago?"

"Great!" Paul looked excited.

Mary shook her head, "Not great. I could barely hear him. His blood counts were a little worse. He wasn't t all sure he could make it in again." She dabbed at her eyes with a tissue. "I really wanted this one to work."

Chapter 15

Pastor Wallace Strinch studied his secretary of many years as she walked down the church aisle. "LouElla, you're walking differently today. No limp. Has something changed?"

LouElla Parsons smiled from ear to ear. "I wasn't going to say anything about it since I didn't want to offend your beliefs about divine healing today. But now that you mention it, yes, I've been healed of arthritis in my hip after 15 years of pain. To me it's a miracle."

"How did this happen?" He stared at her, waiting for an answer. Was she going to blaspheme the Scriptures?

She backed up a step. "I'm sorry, Pastor, but I went to that new place in the mall, that Prayer Place. I figured it was worth a try. My doctor said an artificial hip was the only thing left that'd help me. It'd be extremely painful, take weeks to recover, and our insurance won't pay for much of it. Now it's healed!" She grinned.

"And does it claim to be a Christian place? Do they have Bibles? Did they quote scripture?"

"Oh yes, of course. I don't remember which scriptures they quoted, but they offered me a sheet with a collection of healing scriptures."

"Did you take it?"

She blushed. "No, I was so excited that the pain's gone and no limp that I forgot it."

Strinch paused. "I see. Well, I'm glad you seem better. We'll observe how long it lasts."

"Yes, of course, Pastor." She turned and walked away. He wasn't sure. Did she wipe her eye?

***

"Hi, can I help you? Are you here for prayer?" Mary asked the man in the dark suit and white shirt, carrying a Bible.

Pastor Strinch scrutinized her, then spoke with authority. "No, certainly not. Not at all. But I have heard about this place. So I'm here to find out what it's about."

"That's great." Mary paused. "Well, we are new in the mall, and only here for the summer. The way it works is people come in for prayer and we pray for them. We are students from Branham Seminary. We added staff from local churches because we have so many guests." Strinch just looked at her. She paused again. "Ah, would you like to speak to our director? He should be free in a few minutes."

"Yes, yes, I would."

"I'll tell him. May I have your name?"

"Of course. Here's my card." He placed a business card on her desk.

Mary picked it up, read it, and said, "Well, welcome Pastor Strinch. Our director is Paul Shepard. You can have a seat over there. As I said, he should be out soon." She disappeared with the card.

***

Paul came around the corner with the card and walked over to his visitor. "Pastor Strinch? I'm Paul Shepard. Welcome to The Prayer Place." He held out his hand, feeling a little apprehensive.

Pastor Strinch stood with an air of authority, looked at Paul's hand, and gave it a single shake. "How do you do."

"Pastor, Mary said you're interested in what we do here. It's very basic, very simple."

Strinch locked eyes with him. "Where were you ordained Mr. Shepard?"

Paul reared back in surprise, then smiled and nodded. "Oh, I see." He paused. "Let me start by saying that I forgive you."

"Forgive me? For what?" Strinch said, his voice rising.

"Well, Pastor, first you came here under false pretenses. You claimed to want to learn what we're about."

"Yes?"

"May I continue, Pastor? It's clear that you're already familiar with what we're about, or think you are. And you seem hreatened because we pray for healing. And, by the way, many people are healed when we do."

Strinch's face turned red, his lips tight, but he remained silent.

Paul continued, "I think you came here to challenge us, to challenge our right, and probably our biblical authority, to pray for people." He looked the man in the eye. "Is there any truth to that?"

"Harrumph." Strinch broke eye contact for a moment, then glared at him.

"Before we opened up, I was warned that we'd be challenged, maybe even discredited. So I'm not surprised."

Paul stepped back a pace to regard the Pastor. "Pastor, I will not engage in a Biblical or theological debate with you. We have a sheet of scriptures we make available to our guests that we use as our guide and authority in prayer. And I submit that God honors our prayers with many healings, restorations, some new believers, and hope."

By now the rest of the staff had gathered, plus several new guests who'd come in for prayer. They all watched Paul and the visitor.

"I see." Pastor Strinch said through clenched teeth. "Well, thank you for your time." And he strode out.

As the staff surrounded Paul with words of support and praise, he said. "Thank you folks. But he'll be back. He has to."

"Why, Paul?"

He smiled at the group, "Because, my friends, we threaten one of his core beliefs. But when he does, we must remember to extend the love of Christ."

Chapter 16

As Paul headed into work, he pushed open the mall door startled to see a new sign.

AGE LIMIT

*Anyone under the age of 18 visiting Colony Mall must be accompanied by a parent or adult escort 21 years of age or older.

*One parent or adult escort (21 years of age or older) is permitted to supervise up to 8 youths. Youths under 18 must remain within the company of their adult.

*Visitors are responsible to carry acceptable proof of age (i.e. photo ID with date of birth, including driver's license, state ID, military or college ID, passport or visa).

*Failure to comply with this policy could result in arrest for trespass and arraignment in Juvenile Court.

Thank you for your cooperation.

The sign was repeated in Spanish. Paul spotted a friend of his who worked there as a private security guard. "Hey Jerry, what's with this?"

"Oh!" Jerry smiled. "Got your attention didn't it? It's on all the doors."

"Sure did. Are there problems here?"

"So far, not a lot. But management wants to get ahead of the game. You know teens contact a lot of malls, and some places have real problems with gangs, fights, even some shootings. We're lucky here. We don't have organized gangs, like the Crips or the Latin Kings. But here we've got a couple of groups of teenagers who like to hang out." He continued to survey people as they entered the mall while he talked.

"They don't have a lot to spend, and they get restless. So they roam around, intimidate people—like seniors and young mothers. And pester the girls, and wander through stores. We suspect some petty shoplifting. We don't want them to think of the mall as their social hall; a place to hang out."

"Hm," Paul said, "Sounds right. How will you enforce it?"

"We'll station ourselves near the entrances and turn the kids around if they come in without an escort."

"That should work. Who are these kids? Do you know?"

"I think they're local, from the nearby high schools. One group is Hispanic, the other of a darker persuasion."

"Hm, I wonder if they need prayer," Paul muttered to himself.

Jerry laughed. "I bet they all do. The question is, 'would they come for it?'"

"At that age? I doubt it. I wouldn't have."

"Me neither."

***

Blade, aka Deshawn Silver, strolled up to the mall door, read the sign, and smiled. He was the informal leader of a group with little money and lots of testosterone. Blade admired his own tall stature in his reflection in the door—long, sinewy arms, and skinny jeans. He glanced through the door and spotted a rent-a-cop on the other side. Since the other guys hadn't arrived, he walked over to the bus stop.

Minutes later, four of them filed off the bus. "Hey Blade, what's so funny?" Shaft asked.

Blade grinned. "If I didn't know better, I'd say the mall people here don't like us. There's a sign on the door that we now have to be over seventeen, or escorted by an adult over twenty-one to enter the mall."

"Or what?" Shaft said, aka Tyrell Sabatini. Shaft was the smartest of the bunch, smarter than Blade, short, squat, and light skinned—he often passed for white.

"Or they kick us out, I guess. I'm nineteen, but none of you guys are eighteen—right?"

"Right. What a bummer. That sucks. What're we gonna do?" They all looked at him.

He smiled. "No problemo, hombre. How many rent-a-cops are there at one time?"

"I dunno. Maybe four?"

"Most shifts it's three, plus a city cop after 4:00 Friday, and on the weekend."

"So?"

"So how many doors are there to the mall?"

The boys' faces changed from frowns to smiles. "I dunno, but more than four." Spade said.

"Far more." Blade paused, "Tell you what. Why don't we squeeze into my wheels, take a tour around the mall? Let's see where they put their rent-a-cops—and where they didn't." He spun on his heel and strode through the lot to his Honda Civic. Three in the back seat was tight, but no complaints. When they go to Sears' single door to the parking garage it looked deserted. Blade stopped. "Everyone out. Wait until I park."

Minutes later they filed through the door. Blade kept his voice low. "We need to stay away from the doors and try not to call attention to ourselves. How about the food court? Anybody besides me hungry?"

"Wait a minute!" Devon said. "Did you read that notice? We could be arrested."

Blade laughed. "Hey, chill man. That's if you give them a super hard time, become a repeat offender, or do something real stupid in there. Be cool. They just want to scare you."

The food court was on the second level at the end of the mall. They went up an interior stair to avoid the escalator near a major entrance. After they got what food they could afford, Blade asked, "Anybody seen that Prayer Place downstairs? Down near Macy's?" Nobody answered. "I don't know nothing about it, don't care, either. But I saw some nice chicks in there a couple days ago."

"Alright. Let's go get prayed for—or whatever," Shaft said.

A few minutes later, after a quiet walk through the length of the mall and down another set of stairs, they stood outside the glass front of The Prayer Place.

Mary sat at the desk, talking to some girl.

Blade looked at his group and saw smiles and several thumbs up. He pushed open the door and they all followed. "Good evening, my lucky ladies. How you all doin' tonight?"

Mary looked up with a forced smile. Jaslyn slipped past the group and disappeared into a room toward the back. Mary looked around as she spoke. "Fine, thank you. Are you here for prayer, guys?"

"No way babe. Hey, we're here for you!" Blade blurted out. A man stuck his head out of a prayer room, glanced at the group, snatched up his cell phone and disappeared. Blade stepped forward. "Easy, my man. This is a quality lady." He turned to Mary, "Please, excuse his enthusiasm."

Mary sat back in her chair and folded her arms. This time she was very firm and deliberate. "Well, if you're not here for prayer, then why are you here?"

Blade leaned over and put his hands on the table. "We're only interested in a little sociability, maybe a little action later." He smiled at her. "I'm sure you'd find it very enjoyable."

Blade felt a crushing grip on his shoulder. "I don't think so," a deep voice spoke behind him. He turned around to look up at the biggest man he'd ever seen. The guy was nearly seven feet tall with a hand the size of a catcher's mitt, and a grip like iron. The rest of him was equally massive.

Mary smiled for the first time. "This is Tiny. Tiny used be the right tackle for the Cincinnati Bengals before he came to the Lord. Now he helps us out sometimes." She glanced at Jas. "Thanks, Jas." Jas responded with a thumbs up.

Blade squirmed out of Tiny's grip and looked out the door to the mall. "Oh, no."

Two security guards, and the city police officer were lined up as Jerry waved. Paul waved back. Was this the last of them?

Chapter 17

As Vestal exited her Honda Sybil slipped out her front door and came down the porch steps, holding the handrail. "Vestal, you look ravishing as usual. How are you?"

"I'm fine, but the question is, how are you? You're look a little peaked and I notice you walk kind of slow. Is everything okay"

"Ah, I guess. First trimester. Morning sickness is worse than the first time." She put her hand on Vestal's arm, "I'll be okay. I promise not to upchuck in your car." She forced a smile. "I want to do this. I haven't been out in days. Not to worry, girl, I'm up for it."

Vestal helped her into the low seat, "Good, so am I. You let me know if we need to stop." She closed the door for her.

"How're we gonna' to go about this? This is all new to me."

"Well, today is the easy part. We'll check out the place, see how it's laid out, and the staff–how many, how old, is there any security on site, cameras, and so forth." Vestal backed out of Sybil's drive, and turned toward the highway. "I don't think it'll take very long. Just be natural. We show up as curious tourists-don't get to the mall often, saw this new place—that sort of thing."

"That won't be hard. I guess it's the next visit that will be tricky."

"Yup. I hope we'll be able to devise a scheme to shut them down forever. Vacate the mall. Go back to their ticky-tacky little white churches in the country to sing their schmaltzy songs and whatever!" Vestal tromped on the accelerator.

"Chill girl, we'll figure this out."

**

After a stop in the ladies room, the witches ambled to the Prayer Place. Mary was visible at the reception desk, helping a couple with some forms. They entered and stood behind the couple.

Mary looked up and smiled, "Welcome, ladies. I'll be with you in a minute." She didn't seem to be disturbed by Sybil's facial studs and rings, nor Vestal's alabaster skin.

Sybil whispered. "I need to sit." They took a couple of chairs in the waiting area. An older woman sat next to Sybil and leaned over. "Are you girls here for prayer?"

Sybil shook her head. "No, no. I don't get out to the mall very often, and my friend here told me she'd seen this place. So we thought we'd drop in to see what it's all about." Sybil looked at the woman's round, smiling face and twinkling eyes and asked, "I guess you're here for them to pray about something?"

"Not this time, although it could happen. God works in mysterious ways you know. No," she smiled, "I'm part of the prayer team.

"My last pregnancy, the fifth, was very rough. First, I got preeclampsia. You know, they didn't seem to know a lot about it, and it can be fatal. But between the doctors and a lot of prayer, it ended. Then I was diagnosed with celiac disease. It's also supposed to be incurable. But after I was supernaturally healed of it too I became a real believer in God's power to heal."

She paused and looked at Sybil. "That was years ago, dear. They predicted the most dire things for me and my baby. Well, long story short, my baby is now a fine young man and about to become a father himself, one hundred percent healthy. There have been so many miraculous healings since that time I've lost count." She rotated around to face Sybil, "Oh! Please excuse my rudeness. I'm Loretta, Loretta Youngman." She held out her hand to shake.

Sybil sat back and examined the woman. Was she for real? This lady looked like her long dead grandmother. Sybil felt a little sick to her stomach. She took Loretta's hand with a weak grip. "I'm Sybil."

"Are you alright, dear? Would you like me to pray for you?"

Vestal interrupted. "No! The receptionist is free now. We need to talk to her." She stood up and almost pulled Sybil to her feet. She hissed into Sybil's ear. "What is with you? That lady is not your friend. We're here to stop all this God stuff."

They stepped over to Mary's desk. "Sorry for the delay, ladies. The word is out and we are busy, busy." She put a couple of forms on clipboards at the edge of her desk. "If you're here for prayer, we'd like you to fill these out so we can begin to get to know you."

Vestal responded. "Oh no. I saw this place and told my friend about it. We're a little curious about what goes on here."

Sibyl backed up a couple of steps.

Mary smiled again and looked both of them in the eye. "That's fine. We're so new we don't have any brochures or anything like that, or even website yet. The way it works is we pray for people–pretty much whatever they want, as long as it's in accordance with the Bible, of course. We started last month with four of us from Branham Seminary, and now we have additional volunteers from local churches. I saw you talking to Loretta. She's a volunteer; very nice lady, very experienced, really hears from the Lord."

Sybil smiled again. *Such a nice lady.*

Mary stood up and directed their attention to the back of the store. "This used to be a tax return office, and was almost ideal for our needs with very little work. We took over their conference rooms for prayer. Would you like to meet Paul Shepard, our director?"

Vestal looked at Sybil, who stood mute. "Sure."

"I think he's in the back. Come with me."

Paul stood up as they approached and smiled. "Hey Mary, who do we have here?"

"I'm sorry, The didn't give their names. They say they are curious about who we are and what we do here. I explained it's for prayer, and that we've had lots of healings."

Paul looked at the guests. "That's it, in a nutshell. This is a summer project for our Master's degree, and is turning out to be far more than I expected."

Vestal jumped in, "Summer project? Does that mean you'll be gone in the fall?"

Paul raised his eyebrows. "That's the plan, at least the original plan."

Sybil looked sharply at Vestal and frowned.

Paul continued, "The four of us from Branham will go back to school in September. However, as I said, the way God has moved here so miraculously folks don't want to see it end. So who knows what might happen?" He looked at them both. "May I ask if either of you is associated with a church?"

Both ladies recoiled from his question. Vestal folded her arms and barked, "No! Neither of us."

Paul held out his hands, palms up. "Not even Wiccan?"

Sybil nodded. Vestal spun around without a word and guided Sybil toward the door.

On their way out, Loretta stopped Sybil. "Excuse me dear, but if you don't mind, May I ask you a personal question?"

Sybil didn't see Vestal glare at her when she mumbled, "Okay."

"How far along are you?"

Sybil eyes opened wide. "How did you know about that?" She looked down at her loose shirt and skirt. "I'm not showing." She paused and said, "almost three months."

Loretta smiled. "I have a way with these things. And as I when I asked the Lord to show me anything about it, what I got was that you're having a rough time. Is that right?"

Sybil nodded, unable to speak.

"May I pray for you—and your baby? Just for a moment. We can do it out here." She rested her hand on Sybil's arm. Vestal jerked her other arm toward the door. When Sybil yanked out of her grip, Vestal stomped off to wait by the door.

Whoa. Sybil, wasn't so sure. When she hesitated, Loretta took that as assent, moved her hand gently on Sybil's abdomen, and said, "Lord, this lady needs your gentle loving touch and healing of her distress. I command all morning sickness to go—now, never to return. And I command the baby to be born healthy and robust, with a wonderful future and come to know You. In Jesus name. Amen." Loretta looked in Sybil's eyes. "Thank you, dear. You come back any time."

Thank goodness Vestal didn't notice Sybil mouth, "Thank you," to Loretta, and wipe away a tear as she dragged her out into the mall.

As they left Vestal said, "I think I know how we can shut
down this place."

***

Afterwards, Mary asked Paul, "Wiccan?"

"Witches, Mary, Wiccan is a pagan, nature worshipping outfit. Those two were conducting surveillance."

Mary grabbed Paul's hand. "Oh, Paul."

He slipped his hand out and gave her a sideways shoulder hug. "Not to worry, Mary. Please let me know right away if either one comes back."

Chapter 18

Eddy shuffled along the bleak corridor as he read apartment name plaques. He put his hand on the wall to steady himself. "Please God," he whispered. The next tag read 'Martin Hastings'. That's it! "Thank you." He pressed the button below it. After a short wait something moved at the eyehole. Then the door opened enough to peer out.

"Hi, ah, Eddie–right?"

Eddie nodded and leaned against the door frame.

Marty opened the door all the way. "Man, are you okay? I gotta' tell you, you look like crap."

"I feel like crap, Marty. I hate to do this, but I need help. I'd have called you, but I don't have your number. I need to go back to that Prayer Place, and I can't do it by myself anymore." He paused and looked up, "Any chance you help me get there?"

Marty frowned and hesitated, "Yeah, yeah I guess so. When do you want to go?"

"How about now?"

"Oh man," Marty winced, then proclaimed, "Sure, what the heck. Why not? Sure, let's go. What do you need?"

Eddie smiled a little, and his shoulders relaxed. "Cool, thanks so much. I can hardly walk anymore, and they delivered a wheel chair yesterday." He took a deep breath and looked at Marty with watery eyes. "To be honest, I'm too weak to unpack it and set it up. Could, could you see if you can do it?"

Marty seemed to consider it and rubbed his chin. "Sure, how hard can it be? Lemme take a look."

"Oh man, thank you. Thank you so much. As you can tell, I'm not doin' so hot here. This helps a lot."

***

Thirty minutes later Marty pushed Eddie up to the Prayer Place door. Mary ran up to hold it open for them. "Hi!" She pointed her finger at him. "Eddie!"

Eddie nodded. *Wow, she remembered my name.*

"I'm glad you've got help. I like your new chair." She motioned them to the waiting area. "I'll get the form and help fill it out for you." She bent down to his face level. "I guess you've been having a difficult time. I am so sorry."

"Yeah, yeah I have." He looked back at her and tried to smile. "This is Marty, by the way. My neighbor. I kind of shanghaied him to help me. Wouldn't have made it without him."

"Hi, Marty. So glad you can help. I think the Lord will do real wonders with Eddie today."

Marty looked around and made a face. "Whatever. I'm just here to help. I don't know nothing about this churchy stuff."

Mary smiled again. "Oh, we're not a church. We're here to pray for people." She pulled out a form and attached it to a clip board. "Tell me, Marty, do you believe in God?"

"Yeah, I guess so." He wrinkled his lip. "Don't think about it much."

"Well, in prayer we simply talk to God. He wants everyone to be healthy, and live long, abundant lives you know." She straightened up, filled out a clipboard, and said, "I'll get this to the prayer team right away. I'll put in 'total healing' for your prayer request. Is that okay, Eddie?"

Eddie nodded. After she left Marty said, "These folks sure don't think small do they?"

Eddie nodded again and closed his eyes. Soon afterward he felt a gentle hand on his arm. "Eddie, are you okay?" He opened his eyes to see Paul look at him, with a slight frown.

"Yeah, I'm okay.' His words were slow and faint. "Just resting, Paul." He stopped talking and seemed to gather some strength. "After I came last time, I felt better, even if my counts were worse." He stopped and wiped his eyes.

Then he looked Paul straight in the face. "Paul, this is it. The doctor is talking hospice now, make me comfortable—but not better. Man, I don't want to die! I am not ready to die. This isn't right! This isn't supposed to happen. If this God of yours is real, this has to stop." He held his head and sobbed, tears leaked through his fingers.

Paul squatted next to Eddie's chair and held him in a sideways hug, silent. Mary handed Paul some tissues, which he put in Eddie's hands. After a few moments Eddie blew his nose and wiped his face. "Sorry, man. Thanks."

"No problem, Eddie. That's fine. Of course you have tears. I'm glad you haven't given up. You came here. Excellent. God wants everyone to be healthy." Paul looked around and saw the other guests watch them—and listen. As he stood up and prepared to wheel Eddie into a prayer room, he announced, "I don't know if any of you came in before Eddie, but I feel we need to continue this with him right now."

An older man said, "You go right ahead son."

Paul asked Marty to take a seat in the waiting area, and wheeled Eddie into a prayer room. "This is Julius, Eddie, from a local church, and I guess you remember Jaslyn." Paul asked, "Eddie, do you mind if I anoint you with oil? There is a scripture about this. It says, 'Is anyone among you sick? Let them call the elders of the church to pray over them and anoint them with oil in the name of the Lord. And the prayer offered in faith will make the sick person well; the Lord will raise them up. If they have sinned, they will be forgiven.' Eddie, Julius here is an experienced elder of a local church, and Jas and I function as elders."

Paul removed a small vial from his pocket, screwed off the cap, and waved it under Eddie's nose. "This is frankincense scented olive oil from the Holy Land. May I anoint you with it?" Eddie nodded, and Paul daubed a bit on his finger and touched Eddie's forehead, and the backs of his hands. "Eddie, I anoint you in the name of the Father, the Son, and the Holy Spirit. Remember it says 'make the sick person well,' not only better, but well. The Bible's promises are all true."

Twenty-five minutes later, after prayer and an explanation of how divine healing can work, Eddie smiled at them, his first real smile in days. "Thanks, guys. Thanks a lot. I sure hope Marty is still waiting."

Marty eyes opened wide and his mouth dropped as Eddie came around the corner in his wheel chair. "Wow! You look 1000 percent better. Are you okay now?" Paul and Jaz looked at each other, not smiling.

Eddie said, "I don't know. Actually, my body's about the same, but inside I feel much better. It's hard to explain. Something's happening, that's for sure." He held up a paper. "They gave me these Bible verses to read and say over myself every day. And I need to buy a Bible. I wonder if there's a bookstore in this mall?"

Chapter 19

Kamal watched the Prayer Place activities day after day from his leather goods kiosk. He even scheduled his time now to coincide with their hours of operation. Their business, or whatever they called it, was very popular. More and more people showed up every day. Sometimes they even gathered in the mall before it opened at noon. He recalled what his Muslim Brotherhood trainers said back in Palestine, "Infidels—you must all die! Allahu Akbar!"

He tried to talk to his Uncle Ahmed about it and get his help with the bomb. But his uncle turned soft. He no longer believed. Now he even suggested that they both take the class to become American citizens. He was amazed, and disappointed.

Kamal's friend, Yasir, believed as he did. But Yasir was young, inexperienced. Kamal's anger boiled inside, more every day. He saw these people go in, some with canes or walkers, or even a wheelchair. They looked pathetic, like all infidels. But later, they'd come out and were happy. Many carried their canes or even pushed their own wheelchairs. A few stopped at his kiosk to browse through the merchandise and perhaps buy something. He struggled to look at them.

While he straightened up his stock he remembered what his mother taught him in Madrassa as a child. The Koran's truth that the street should run red with the blood of

Jews and Christians. And for a believer to die as *al-shayeed,* an Islamic martyr, was the surest way to earn a place in Paradise. His blood surged and adrenaline seized his entire body when he thought about this.

And the fear, the fear gripped him too. What did he do? Zip. Absolutely nothing. Sure, he'd watch Imams on the Internet rail against the wicked ways of the West. He forced himself to turn away from all the women with their bare faces, and the girls in their short shorts, and gaudy makeup. But he admitted to himself that he often paused before did—that he was a needy and lonely young man.

It must be Allah who had put him here in front of this ungodly place with their prayer and music and supposed miracles. This was not by chance, not an accident. But he was only one man. He couldn't kill all these people. Could he even kill the young people there who prayed? Not likely. And now older people did it too. Sometimes they'd stop and chat with him. He hated it when they asked him if he wanted prayer, wanted to come in. He tried to be polite when he said, "No, thank you," but he never revealed how intensely he despised them, how his stomach cramped when they asked him.

How about their store? If he wrecked that, they would have to stop. They might go some place else. That'd be better. At least then Kamal wouldn't have to see it every day. He'd find the best place to put a bomb, one that caused the most destruction and close them down. It must be inside, near the door. But if it was near the door what about damage to his kiosk? A little damage might not be bad, but not a lot.

And how to fuse it so they wouldn't find it, render it useless or take it outside? He'd peeked inside their door many times and saw they had hardly any furniture. No obvious place to hide a bomb. But they'd never know if he put it in at night. He'd use a time delay detonation so he and Yasir escaped before it went off.

He'd have to pay more attention to how they unlocked the front door when they opened up. Since they always unlocked from the inside, they had a back door. So there must be a service corridor in back of the stores along there. He'd have to find the entrance. Maybe he'd ask the mall manager if there was some place beside his kiosk where he might store his stock. That might help him get access to the back.

And this guy, Paul, was so persistent and so darned friendly too—and gentle. He seemed to want to know about Kamal, be his friend. Paul knew he was Muslim, not Christian. He and Paul were about the same age. But Kamal was bigger, and undoubtedly stronger. He wondered if Paul ever had any combat training. He remembered his mother taught him that one Muslim man had the strength of ten infidels.

Paul told him that The Prayer Place was his idea. It was a project for his university. What kind of university gave credit for this? None that Kamal ever heard of.

As he sorted a shipment of belts he sensed movement from The Prayer Place. Paul came out smiling like an idiot. Maybe, if the bomb didn't work out, he should just kill him.

Chapter 20

"Are you ready for this? Got the game plan?" The shorter man whispered to his conspirator as they approached The Prayer Place.

"Not to worry," his partner smirked as he reached for the door.

***

Mary came up to Paul, but didn't interrupt him, talking to the new prayer team members.

"Oh no, excuse me folks." He turned to her. "Mary, what've we got here?" She was holding two guest information forms.

"Sorry to interrupt, Paul, but these two men came in together and wouldn't say much about why they are here." She looked in his eyes, "You know sometimes I get a feeling about some of our guests. I can't explain it, but I don't think I'm supposed to ignore it. I hope this is okay even if you're not up next in the regular prayer rotation."

Paul gave her a shoulder hug and returned her look. "Mary, it's fine. Say, did I ever tell you how glad I am that you are part of our team?"

She looked down, then put her hand on Paul's arm. "No, not explicitly. Thanks Paul."

He squeezed her hand. "Well, I do. I put a lot of faith in these 'feelings' you get. You have real spiritual sensitivity—

besides being a wonderful person." He grinned at her and took the two forms. "Okay, who are these guys?" He studied them a moment. "Hm, same address for both of them. In fact, these forms are almost identical." He looked over her shoulder towards the waiting room. "They in there?"

She nodded.

"Okay, I've got the ball. Good quarterbacking. Can you get Julius to pray with me on this one. It's a guy thing. I'll meet him in prayer room two please?"

She nodded again as Paul took the forms to the waiting area.

"Anton and Hank?" Two men stood up. "Hi, I'm Paul Shepard. I will be praying for you today."

The tall one wore tight khaki pants, a knit shirt and leather shoes, well shined. He was over six feet, with a thin, narrow face, high cheekbones, and silky smooth skin. Paul wondered if he used makeup. His bottle blond hair fell over his ears and almost down to his shoulders. He had a gold chain around his neck, and rings on a couple of fingers.

The second one was well short of six feet, also in tight khaki pants. His broad shoulders and sleeves slid up to the elbows on his sweater to expose his powerful forearms. This guy must have spent a lot of time in the gym or weight room. Paul spotted a tattoo poking out of the left sleeve. His dark brown, unkempt hair curled around his ears, offsetting a gold ring in the right one. His unpolished deck shoes revealed tan, bare ankles.

He advanced his hand. "Hi, Hank. Hank Polaski"

Paul braced for a bone-crushing grip, which didn't disappoint.

Paul looked at the tall one. "Then you must be Anton," and reached out his hand. Anton's handshake was almost flaccid.

He took them to the prayer room and introduced Julius. "We always work in a team. Most times two, since we're so busy lately, but sometimes more." Then he stopped and looked at them. "Okay, gentlemen, why are you here? What can we do for you?"

They glanced at each other. Anton spoke in a soft voice, "Well, we met several years ago and have grown quite fond of each other. So for some time we've been talking about moving to the next stage, formalizing our relationship. We both consider ourselves Christians although we're not in a church right now. We know that this is controversial in the church, but the one opinion that counts to us is God's. So we would like prayer to determine that."

Paul folded his hands, stepped back, took a deep breath. "I want to be sure I understand your request. You are asking us to pray to find out if it's okay with God for you to marry each other–is that right?"

They both nodded in agreement. Hank slipped his hand into Anton's.

"I see. Well, I'm glad you want to know God's opinion. I hope you believe, as we do, that the Bible is the most explicit expression of his will and character. This place, this Prayer Place, is Christian. We follow the precepts in the Holy Bible. You may be aware that there are several scriptures that deal with this subject.

Hank barked, "Hey, that's all Old Testament. Didn't Jesus cut a new deal?"

Paul and Julius both smiled. Paul nodded to Julius, who said, "Mr. Polaski, that's not quite accurate. First, Jesus came to fulfill the law, not to repeal it all. And second, the New Testament is clear on this subject. He lifted his Bible and thumbed to a page. "Hank, if you would be so kind, read a couple of lines from Paul's letter to the Romans, Chapter 1, starting with verses twenty six and seven. Aloud please."

Hank took the Bible, looked at Anton with pleading eyes, and then at the page. He read clearly, but barely audibly.

'For this reason God gave them up to vile passions. For even their women exchanged the natural use for what is against nature.

Likewise also the men, leaving the natural use of the woman, burned in their lust for one another, men with men committing what is shameful, and receiving in themselves the penalty of their error which was due.'"

Anton pursed his lips and looked at Hank with a frown. "Hm, that's a new one to me." He held his hand out to Hank. "May I see that?"

Hank handed over the Bible. Paul said, "Anton, this is not the only mention. There are more references in the New Testament. So, gentlemen, the answer is 'no', we will not pray for that. God's position is already clear. However, we'd love to pray for other things for you if you like. "

All four men stepped back and were silent. After a long pause Hank said, "Well, I guess that's that." He looked up at Anton, who frowned. "You ready?"

Paul said, "I realize this is not the answer you'd hoped for, but before you go can I ask you both a question?"

They nodded acceptance.

"Is either one of you dealing with HIV?"

"Yeah, I am." Anton's answer was so soft he was hard to hear. He looked at Paul with glistening, drooping eyes.

Paul kept his voice soft and low. "I am so sorry. Is it AIDS yet?"

"No, not yet. But the treatment doesn't seem to be working. They say I've got a new strain."

"Would you like prayer for it? That is something we could do. In fact, we'd like to."

"You would do that?" Anton seemed amazed. "Even after that scripture condemns us?"

"Of course. Jesus loves you. There is none righteous, no, not one. Hey, he healed people of leprosy, even blindness.

HIV wasn't around then, but I'm sure he'd have no problem with it." Paul grinned.

Anton said, "Okay, sure," and stepped forward.

"May I anoint you with oil?"

Anton's eyes glistened, "Please."

When Paul and Julius finished praying, Paul said, "Some healings are instantaneous. We get them fairly often here. But my sense about you is that yours will be progressive. It will take time. So my question is how are you going to tell if you're getting better?"

Anton shrugged, and stuck out his lower lip, "Easy, I test. If my counts start going down, it's working. If not ..." Hank put his hand on Anton's arm and gave a gentle squeeze."

"Do you have to go to the doctor for this? Is it difficult?"

"Oh no, I get home test kits. I order four packs of them from Amazon. They're a little pricey, as I recall thirty-eight a pop. But I don't even have to stick my finger any more–just a cheek swab. Results in twenty minutes or so." Anton seemed more animated than any time since he got there. "In fact, I will take one when I get home."

Hank frowned and looked at him.

Anton looked back. "Hey, why not? Why not find out if it's working?"

Paul said, "It feels like we're about done, but before you go, could I ask for a favor? One problem we have here is that we pray for lots of people, and many times never hear from them again. They walk out the door, and unless they come back, which a good number do, we don't know what happened. So could you call us with your test results?"

"Sure, why not?" He looked at Hank. "You got the number?" Hank shook his head.

"I'll give you a card. And if you think you're getting better, in your case I'd very much recommend that you come back for more prayer."

"Count on it Paul. And if it works you can count on seeing more cases."

Paul laughed. "That's fine. Bring 'em on!"

Minutes later Paul asked Julius, "So, will they call?"

Julius shook his head. "Depends on the results. Good news, yup. Bad news, doubtful. But then I worry about that Hank guy making trouble for us."

"Me too."

Chapter 21

"Doc, you gotta' be kidding. You want me to do what?" Anthony "Tony" Ziparelli, attorney at law, reclined in his high-backed leather chair with a wide grin, the phone tucked next to his ear.

"I'm serious, Tony, those kids cost me money. I just had my third surgery cancellation since they started up—cancellation Tony, not delay." Dr. Charles Hudson, Orthopedic Surgeon, sounded very frustrated. "Can you find out if we can sue them for practicing medicine without a license? This has got to stop."

"Charlie, Charlie, Charlie—I do wills, trusts and contracts, even real estate once in a while. I don't know zip about practicing medicine without a license. That's a new one. But why don't you tell me more about this and I'll see what I can do?"

"Okay, first off, are you familiar with this place in the mall where they pray for people?"

"Yeah, it was on Channel 9 a couple of nights ago. A bunch of students from Kentucky, as I recall, opened it up for the summer. Some kind of project." He paused, then continued. "To be honest, it sounded interesting. Knowing me, I wondered who foots the bill for the place. Can't be cheap. I guess the kids are all volunteers."

"Hm. I never wondered who paid for it. I figured we'd get them to stop praying. If I can recover damages, that'd be great. This has already cost me thousands." He looked at his friend. "I run a neighborhood medical practice, most of it Medicare. I don't have the resources of a big consortium of doctors.

"Slow down there, Doc, get a grip. I'll check into it. But I can tell you now that the crux of this will be whether prayer can be construed as practicing medicine."

He heard his friend's breathing, but no words. Then, "Nuts. You're probably right, Tony. But there has to be something we can do."

"Okay, Doc, Let me check around and I'll call you in a couple of days."

"Thanks. That's all I ask. Find me something, anything."

Tony's grin was replaced with a slight frown as he rotated his squat body around to gaze out the window. It helped him collect his thoughts. He rubbed his chin, smiled, swiveled back to the desk, checked his Rolodex, and reached for the phone.

***

"Dr. Hudson, a Mister Ziparelli is here. He doesn't have an appointment." The receptionist read from a business card which she placed on his desk.

"No problem, Susan. Show him in."

Charlie rose to greet him. "Tony, what a pleasant surprise. I hope it doesn't mean bad news." They shook hands and sat in the Doctor's consultation chairs. "How about coffee, a Coke, something stronger?"

"No, I'm good." Tony grinned at his friend. "I decided I'd make a house call for a change. I find face to face makes it easier to explore options too." He squared away to study the doctor. "Let me ask you a couple of questions. First, did any of your patients report that they were told by the student that they could cancel their surgery?"

Charlie bit his lip for a moment. "No, not that I recall."

"Hm, too bad. That'd have been the best. Now ..." Tony stopped in mid sentence, as Charlie held up his hand.

"In fact, Mrs. Simmons told me they said she should check with her doctor to be sure she was healed." He pursed his lips. "And she was. When I first saw her she was so crippled up she could hardly function. And when she came back this last time she might have played the harp with those fingers." He looked at Charlie, eyebrows raised. "Sounds like a miracle doesn't it?"

Tony sighed. "Well, I don't know about miracles. But, yes, it sounds very remarkable." He folded his arms. "Okay, I talked to a buddy of mine who has handled a few of these cases. He was very helpful. What we need is evidence that will stand up in court that they dispense medical advice. Like if they told a client that they no longer needed their medication. Or in your case, surgery."

"When donkeys fly! How am I going to get that? This isn't help Tony."

Tony shook his head. "I realize it's not. In fact, it gets worse. I told my buddy about the mall place and your cancelled surgeries. He's never tried a case like this, but he knows of a few of these faith healing cases on the books. He hadn't heard of any of them that won.

The doctor's shoulder slumped, the picture of despair.

"Charlie, how serious are you about this?"

"Pretty darn serious. As I said, it's already cost me thousands, and can easily be much more. But what options do we have?"

"Well, there's one thing that comes to mind."

Charlie leaned forward in his chair. "Which is?"

"We might, ah, encourage them to give medical opinions." Tony sat back to regard his host. "We could send in someone, or call on the phone, with proper documentation equipment, pose some medical situation, and ask for their advice."

"You mean wear a wire?" Charlie's voice rose as he spoke.

"In a word—yes." Tony waited a moment for his friend to settle down. "Charlie, you said you were serious. We need to be creative here."

"Man, I'm not sure about that." He slammed his fist into his palm. "I don't feel I'm ready to try a stunt like this." He looked at Tony, appeared to study him. "And even if this worked, if we could get this kid in court. What then? Send him to jail? For praying for people? I don't think so. Shut down his store?" He shook his head.

"You make a good point, Charlie. A lot would depend on how this showed up in the media. I mean, the coverage the other night was very favorable. What you want them to do is quit—right?"

Charlie nodded.

Tony reached out his hand to calm the doctor. "Look, Doc, let's do this. You don't have to do a thing. In fact, I can keep your name out of it. I want to do a little exploratory work with the place itself—to get a better idea of what and who we are dealing with. The best outcome would be to collect enough of a case to form a charge. Then we negotiate an agreement. We settle for a cease and desist order, and they close up shop. No trial, hopefully no media, minimal legal fees. As you said they're students. They won't have much money anyway." He stopped to be sure Charlie followed him. "How does that sound?"

Charlie shook his head back and forth. "I'm not sure, Tony. I guess since you say I don't have to do anything, I won't know squat. Right?"

Tony smiled, "That's right."

Charlie sighed and seemed to relax. "Well, sure. I'll do nothing further on this. That's all you're ask of me."

"Okay, my friend. Stay tuned for the news. Let's see what I can do."

Chapter 22

Eddie looked at his spotted hands trying to move the wheels on his chair. He willed his puffy fingers to have the strength he needed. He'd gotten the apartment door open and started down the hall to Marty's apartment. Marty said he'd drive Eddie again, although without much enthusiasm. That was okay. At least he said he'd do it.

He rapped on Marty's door and waited. He tried to sit up straight in the chair, but gave up. Too darned hard.

Marty came out and stepped behind Eddie's chair. "All set?"

"Yup."

"What are the bags for?"

Eddie held up a handful of plastic bags. "I don't want to mess up your car, or go on the floor in the mall. I can't keep much down the last couple of days."

"Oh man, that's rough. Are you sure you're up to this?"

"I have to be Marty, I have to be. This is the last game in town." Eddie tried to force air and energy into his body.

He appreciated Marty's easy touch as he moved him to his car and opened the door for him. He eased himself up out of the chair and pivoted around to sink back in the car seat. As he was about to lift his legs into the car he sat forward, held his hand up to Marty and pulled out a bag. He gagged and retched for a few moments, then looked at Marty and tried to smile. "Dry heaves. Okay, I'm ready."

As they started out of the parking lot Marty said, "Eddie, I start a day job in a couple of days, so you'll need to find someone else to drive you next time."

"Good for you. No problem. It's like the bottom of the ninth anyway."

"Oh man. That sucks."

"That it does." Eddie nodded.

***

Eddie had no clue how he got from the car to The Prayer Place. Was he dosing? passed out? His first awareness was when Mary opened the door for them.

"Hi, Eddie. I'm so glad you're here."

Eddie looked forward to Mary's gentle manner and soft touch on his shoulder. "Thanks. Mary. Is Paul here? Can he pray for me?"

"I'm so sorry, Eddie. Paul's off for the afternoon."

"Oh no." His last bit of energy was like the final water draining out of a bathtub.

She patted his blotchy hand. "It will be all right. In fact, we try to put repeat guests with different staff. They often get new insights and words of knowledge." She referred to her computer. "I'll put you with Cal and Jaslyn, two of Paul's colleagues from school."

Marty let her push him into a prayer room. As they entered the room Cal and Jas raised their heads, unclasped their hands and said a soft, "Amen." Cal reached out to shake Eddie's hand. "Eddie? I'm Cal, and this is Jas. Paul's told us about you already. How are you this afternoon?"

Eddie must have said something, but he no idea what. The nausea and pain overwhelmed him. But then it faded away as they talked and prayed, like being in a half dream. He heard their words, but didn't care what they said. He closed his eyes to a thick fog, with pale, golden light, and leaned back in his chair, and smiled—for the first time in weeks. Jas mentioned something about hexes, curses, bondages, and generation transfers—whatever that was about. Didn't care. As he sank into his chair and the fog, a new aura of peace enveloped him. It was like fluids ran out his fingers and toes, taking the toxins and pain with them.

Cal put his hand on Eddie's head and muttered under his breath.

Cal's touch was like a warm towel fresh from the dryer. The chill was gone. It began weeks ago. He opened his eyes enough to view his hands. No more ugly spots. Instead—nice, fresh, healthy skin. When he tried to lift his arm and clenched his fist, they felt strong.

Once more he closed his eyes again and sat back. They prayed more, even commanded things to leave his body. He wanted more, more of whatever they did. His body was like a soft balloon character slowly inflating. He moved his shoulders and torso a little, not too much. He could flex his fingers, even his toes. His lungs expanded, held it, and relaxed. Confident that he could draw another deep breath.

This time he opened his eyes wide and grinned at them. They smiled back. Tears ran down Jas's cheeks. She said, "Thank you, Jesus."

He felt his own eyes fill with tears. He tried to say 'Thank you' also, but couldn't talk. Jas pressed a couple of tissues into his hand. He wiped his eyes and blew his nose. "Wow! Thank you Jesus." He looked at them both. "And thank you Cal and Jas. You guys are terrific."

He pursed his lips in thought. "I wonder..." He shifted his weight forward on his chair to try to stand up. Cal reached out to steady him. Eddie waved him off. "No, let me see if I can do this." He flexed his legs and rose from the chair, hanging on to the arm. After a moment he released the arm, stood up straight, and grinned and looked at them. He flashed his eyebrows a couple of times in triumph. "Ah, yes, back on my feet. It's been a while." He was tempted to turn around to see if the floor was covered with whatever he felt drained out of his body, but knew better. He tried a couple of steps and grabbed Cal's shoulder. "Sorry man, not so steady yet." But he wasn't ready to sit down. He rested one hand against the wall, and lifted one knee, then the other. Again he tried to walk. This time was better. He let go and still made progress. He turned around and shuffled back to his chair. However, instead of sitting, he wheeled it around and gripped the handles, like a walker. "This is going to work. Wait until Marty sees me, and Mary."

Cal spoke up. "Eddie, you need to see your doctor. It's obvious you got a healing here. But he needs to tell you how much, and what to do about medication. Okay?"

"Okay." Eddie answered with little enthusiasm. "I'm ready to drop the chemo right now. It's like prescription Draino."

"I know, but see your doctor first. Will you promise me that?"

"Yessir. I'll do it. And thank you again, both of you."

"You're welcome. We love to do it, but we're only the conduits. Thank Jesus and the Holy Spirit. That's where the power comes from."

Eddie pushed his chair back into the waiting room,.

Marty leaped out of his seat. "No way, man! What happened? Are you on drugs?"

"Yes, too darned many of them. But no drugs from here. I'm on Jesus here. Looks like I just might pull this game out in the ninth."

Chapter 23

Kamal almost cheered as Yasir pulled up in his driveway. He hurried down his back steps to the garage door as he reached for his keys. He noticed Yasir came out of his car empty handed. "Didn't you bring the gunpowder and fuse and stuff."

Yasir smiled and put his hand on Kamal's shoulder. "Oh I have, my friend. They're in my car. First, I want to check out the set-up here before I carry bomb parts out in front of the neighbors."

Kamal felt his face flush. He should have thought of this. "Good thinking. I guess I'm kind of excited." He opened the garage's side door and flipped on the overhead lights. "Here we are. We could use the bench over there. I can lock this place up tight and have already covered the windows. Nobody else can get in here."

"Not even the landlord? You rent, right?"

"Well, yes. But he doesn't come around very often, and never to the garage."

"No sweat. We can lock everything in my trunk when we're done. This looks fine. Oh good, you have a DeWalt drill. Excellent choice." He flipped on the fluorescent light over the bench. "Looks like a decent vise too, although I'm not sure we'll need it." He surveyed the garage floor, and bit his lower lip. "If we're careful, we can even test some components right here." He turned to the door, "Okay, let me get my stuff."

He plopped two plastic bags on the bench and pulled out a green coil of ropy material still wrapped in plastic. The label said 'Cannon Fuse'. The second bag contained a fiber cylinder of gunpowder. Kamal's eyeballs opened wide. "Wow! This is the real stuff. We're actually going to do this. It's hard to believe."

"Easy there, my friend. This is not kid stuff. I want to test the fuse and gunpowder first before we build anything." Yasir slit open the fuse bag with his pocket knife and cut off a section about ten inches long. "Let's test how it burns, how long it takes."

"Okay" Kamal responded. "Got a match?"

"Nope, don't smoke. Do you have one, or a lighter?"

"Oh no. What a couple of amateurs." He frowned. "I don't have one in the house either." He took a deep sigh. "Okay, I'll run down to the convenience store and get a lighter. Back in a few minutes."

"Good, I'll drill the cap for the fuse. Where are your bits?"

Kamal slid the work bench drawer open to reveal drill bits, screw drivers, and some chisels. "Find what you need?"

"I will. See you in a few minutes."

At last Yasir found a drill bit close to the fuse's diameter and held the tip up in the light. It looked like they had used it to build the pyramids. "Hm," he muttered as he turned his attention to the vise. He cranked it open to clamp the pipe cap. Then he drilled a small pilot hole through the center of the cap. But when Kamal returned he was leaning on the drill with both hands with the final bit.

"I got a couple of lighters." He watched Yasir's efforts with the drill. "I guess I don't need to ask about the drilling. Is it supposed to smoke like that?"

Yasir grunted, "No, it shouldn't, but I couldn't find any cutting fluid or oil, and this drill bit is about as sharp as a stick of butter." His bit broke through the last of the pipe cap. "Got it! I'll get a new bit before we try this again." He wiped his brow and took the lighter from Kamal. "Okay, let's see how this burns." He took the fuse to the middle of the garage's concrete floor and squatted down with the lighter. First, he flicked the lighter until he got a steady flame, then put it on the end of the fuse. When the fuse started to sputter Yasir jumped back and studied it. He glanced at his watch.

The fuse burned to the end with no trouble. "About five seconds," Yasir announced.

He smiled at Kamal who grinned in response and exclaimed, "Yes! So, what's next?" He picked up the pipe and tried screwing on the cap. It fit.

"Easy there. Now we need to see how the fuse lights the gunpowder. It'd be a shame to put it all together and no boom."

"Yeah, for sure. What have you got in mind?"

"Well, I've never done this before." He picked up the cylinder of gunpowder. "I'll put a pile of this on the floor, stick a fuse in it, and hope it lights."

"Lights or explodes?"

"Lights. I've read up on this. Gunpowder doesn't explode, but burns fast, real fast. That's why there's a flash out of the barrel of a gun. It's the powder burning." He looked pensive. "At least that's what they say." He pried off the end of the cylinder and peeled off the security seal. Then he poured out about a tablespoonful of the grey, granular material in a small pile in the middle of the floor. "Do I know how much to use for this? Not a clue." He said, as much to himself as to Kamal.

Kamal stood at the bench with the coil of fuse and his knife out. "Same length?"

"No, let's double it. I want to get a better timing idea."

Kamal cut it to about twenty inches and handed it to Yasir, who put one end on the little mound of gunpowder. "Stand back. I'm not sure what'll happen." Once again he got a steady flame on his lighter. "Start timing." He placed the flame under the free end of the fuse and jumped back to the far corner of the garage.

They were fascinated as the flame moved along the fuse toward the gunpowder. All at once it gave a bright flash, a slight whooshing sound, and was all gone but a little smoke.

Kamal clapped his hands. "Beautiful, absolutely beautiful."

"Eighteen seconds," Yasir announced. "Okay, one more test. I want to be sure that the fuse will burn through the hole in the cap." He cut off another length of fuse and threaded it through the hole he'd drilled in the pipe cap. He put the cap in the vise, with the open end up. Then he poured a little gunpowder into the recessed end of the cap until only the end of the fuse poked through. Once again, he lit the lighter, and positioned it at the far end the fuse. The moment it lit he jumped back several feet. This time the fuse burned its way to the pipe cap, disappeared in the hole in the cap, and once again, a pfftt, a whiff of smoke and the gunpowder was gone. "Oh yes!" Yasir said. "Allah be praised."

Kamal threaded the undrilled pipe cap on the pipe and clamped it in the vise. Yasir poured the pipe full of gunpowder and tamped it down, almost emptying the container. He piled a little on the end to fill the second pipe cap. "How much fuse will we need for our test?"

"I'd judge five feet would be enough."

He cut it to length, stuffed one end through his hole, and threaded the cap on the pipe, tightened it as hard as he could with his hands. "I don't suppose you've got a wrench around here someplace?"

Kamal raised his hands, palms up. "Sorry, I don't. Should I get one?"

"No, I guess not. We're don't want to make this watertight anyway do we?"

"Say, aren't we supposed to put in bits of metal, like nuts and screws, to increase the blast damage?"

"Yeah, we should do that for the final one. But for this test I want to find out what the gunpowder alone will do. How soon do you want to test it?"

"How about tomorrow?"

Chapter 24

Dr. Richard Schneider, Academic Dean, and Dr. Nancy Henning, Advisor and Professor to Paul Shepard and his colleagues approached The Prayer Place door.

"Did you tell them we were coming?"

Nancy grinned, "No, I assumed you wanted it to be a surprise."

"I did. We need to observe them in their normal situation. Otherwise they'd get all nervous and want to prepare something for us."

"And this won't make them nervous?" She raised an eyebrow.

"Well," he let out a sly smile, "it's possible." He reached for the door and held it open for her.

Mary leaped to her feet. "Dr. Henning, Dr. Schneider, what a pleasant surprise. Welcome to The Prayer Place." She turned several shades of pink. "Let me tell Paul you're here." She started towards the back of the store.

Nancy reached out and patted her arm. "Relax, Mary. This is just an informal visit. Okay, let's talk to you and Paul together. I take it you're kind of the office manager?"

Mary blushed again, but before she could respond Paul showed up and blurted out, "More like a saving angel. She keeps us on our toes, runs the whole place, puts out fires, and comes up with lots of wonderful suggestions." He moved next to Mary and gave her a sideways hug. She looked like she wanted to melt into his arms. Paul had no clue. Typical man.

"So, what brings you to our little project? How can we help you?" He gestured towards six people waiting. Some filled out their forms on a clip-board. "As you can tell, we're pretty busy."

Richard said, "Paul, your 'little project', as you call it, isn't so little. It was on local television down in Lexington. When the reporter called it 'the miracle store' it really piqued our interest. So Nancy and I decided to come up and see it in the flesh. We don't want to interrupt you. We'd like to observe, and also talk to each of you students, if possible."

Paul seemed to hesitate, then said, "Sure, we can do that. Would you mind if you sit in individually?" He cleared his throat. "Ah, some of our guests come with very personal issues, and might feel inhibited if two strangers watched over their shoulder."

"No problem," Richard said.

Mary pointed to the form she held. "Paul, Anton is here. I've got him scheduled for you and Julius since you saw him the first time."

"He's back. That's great. This must mean his count has gone down." He looked at his visitors. "He had HIV that hadn't responded to medication. But when he came in with his partner, I suspect they came to get started on an LGBT protest. But when we discovered the HIV problem they let us pray for that. Dr. Schneider can join us." He turned to Mary. "Do you have someone for Dr. Henning?"

Mary referred to her computer. "Well, we have a new guest, Aliyah. She says she's here for arthritis. I have Jas and Martha for her. Would that work?"

Nancy said, "Sounds good to me."

Paul took a small step forward. "I assume you're here to look and listen, but not take part in the prayer ministry?"

Nancy said, "Absolutely. Right Richard?"

He nodded. "You're the experts. You do the miracles."

Paul cleared his throat again. "Praise God the Holy Spirit shows up to do that."

Dr. Henning said, "Yes, of course. By the way, you said 'Holy Spirit', not 'God or Jesus.'"

"Yeah. In fact, that's part of the orientation we give new prayer volunteers—to pray in their authority as received from the Holy Spirit. Not to expect Jesus to show up and do it all. He did His part on the cross."

Nancy opened a notebook and started writing. "I need to capture this. It's obvious we have a lot to learn here."

***

Thirty minutes later, both groups emerged from their prayer rooms, the doctors grinned. Richard said, "This is incredible. That guy is actually being healed of HIV."

"And the lady I saw will go home now with no arthritis pain – after years of struggle with conventional medicine." Nancy added.

Richard turned to Paul. "Is this typical?"

He shook his head. "Not all the time. Sometimes it turns out their stated issue is on the surface of something deeper. Sometimes their real need is counseling, which we don't do. And sometimes we pray but no results. Of course it can happen later, but we don't always find out. Anton's return is not that common." He looked at Dr. Schneider. "Okay, do you want to observe some more? Or maybe something else?"

Richard said, "Is there some place Nancy and I could talk with each of you about your experiences here? I realize you're busy but perhaps one at a time. Could you work that in?"

Paul nodded. "I'd say so. Let's check with missions control." They looked puzzled. "That's Mary." He smiled. "How much time do you think you'll need with us?"

The doctors looked at each other. Nancy said, "Fifteen minutes okay?"

Fifteen minutes turned out to be thirty or forty minutes. Paul's interview lasted almost an hour. At the end of his, Richard said, "Paul, this has been remarkable. To be honest, I didn't know what to expect. Right now I'd like a few minutes to consult with Dr. Henning and then meet with the four of you. Is that possible?"

Paul glanced at his watch. "I'm sure it is. Traffic here slows down during the dinner hour, so tell me when you want us. I'll alert the others."

Twenty minutes later they all gathered around a table in the break area. Richard sat at one end, with Nancy next to him. He smiled at the students, who looked a little anxious about what he'd say. "First of all, let us both say you all do a fantastic job. This is a truly remarkable project. As you recall, this was proposed as a Master's project for Paul, with missions credit to the rest of you. But it's obvious that each of you have a unique and profound experience this summer. So Dr. Henning and I agree that if you write up your individual experiences and learnings, we will give you Master's thesis credit."

"All right!" Cal said as he hi-fived Jas.

"I thought that'd go over well. We also have an observation we'd like to pass on." He looked around the group. "People, you are tired. This is hard work, lots of stress. And you don't seem to have much time together to relax and enjoy each other. I've seen this with foreign missionaries in the field, more than once."

Paul said, "You're right. I hadn't realized that. What do you suggest?"

Nancy said, "Take a day off to party. How about a picnic, a trip on the river, a barbeque, a corn hole party—that's for you to say. And we suggest you include all your local volunteers too."

Paul saw Mary smile. "Mary?"

Her eyes sparkled. "Oh, I love to plan parties. Naturally I want to do everything they suggested."

Everyone laughed and relaxed.

Richard said. "Good. Go for it folks. You deserve it. Lastly, we have a problem."

The student's euphoria turned to frowns. Richard said, "We don't want this to stop. The original plan is that you all will come back to campus in the fall, perhaps as celebrities to some extent. And The Prayer Place would close up." He smiled at each of them, one at a time. "What you're doing here is amazing. On a shoestring you are a center for God's work in the marketplace—as Paul's proposal said. I understand that some people drive fifty miles or more for prayer."

He sat back, looked reflective. Nancy said, "So we want to put together a plan to continue The Prayer Place. It might become an on-going project of the University. We might turn it over to a local church. You already have more local people on staff here than from school. We don't know how to do it. We will want to have discussions with the management of the mall, and with Paul's parents whose generous donation of this facility made it all possible. And we want your ideas. You four are the experts, not us."

Cal raised his hand. "May I make a suggestion?"

"Please."

"Isn't there one more source to consult?"

"Which is?"

"God."

Chapter 25

Mary backed into a spot near the park shelter, popped the trunk, and jumped out of the car as Jas came around the other side. "I'm so glad we could reserve this shelter. They told me it was booked for weeks, but somebody cancelled the morning I called."

Jas looked around, "Yeah, it looks ideal. Plenty of parking, close to a ball field, horseshoe pit, and the restrooms are even close."

They continued to chat as they spread a plastic tablecloth and unloaded the food as a second car pulled up. "Oh, good, here are the guys from Fresh Fire. Julius is grilling the burgers and dogs."

"No brats?" Jas asked. "Didn't Paul say he loved brats?"

"Yep. Of course, brats. Gotta' keep the boss happy," Mary said.

"Yeah, I saw you put a good bit of attention to the 'keeping the boss happy' department."

Mary blushed. "You picked up on that, huh? Do you think Paul did?"

Jas pursed her lips, "Not so sure about that. Sometimes he needs a little nudge. He tends to be intense."

"Well, as we were saying." Several cars rolled to a stop, led by Paul and Cal.

"Beautiful ladies of The Prayer Place," Paul said with a broad smile. "Mary, this is wonderful. How did you do it so fast?"

"Thanks, Paul. I have a secret weapon."

"Which is?"

"Delegate, delegate, delegate."

They all laughed as Jas and Julius nodded in agreement. "She does do that." Paul said, "Like a pro."

"In this case, it was easy. Dr. Schneider was right on when he said we needed a break, to party. People volunteered with no sales pitch. The Fresh Fire people know the town, this park, and what's available. They also have garages and basements full of corn hole boards, horse shoes, and softball equipment."

Paul asked, "And Frisbees? I hope."

Mary frowned, "I'm not sure about that. I missed that one since I don't play it."

Paul feigned a shocked expression. "Life without Frisbee? Hardly worth living. We'll correct that today. I have a sack full in my trunk."

Mary blushed. "I didn't realize, Paul. It's hard to imagine. Sure, I'd love to try it, if you can teach me." She looked at him and felt her pulse pick up.

"With pleasure. For once it will be my turn to show you something. You ready to try it?"

Mary's heart fell. "Paul, sure, but not now. Jas and I are doing the food. Can we do it after lunch?"

Paul seemed less interested. "Yeah, I guess so. Sure, lunch has to come first."

Mary blushed when she realized that an audience of arriving people overheard their little conversation, some of them with sly smiles. Her heart had leapt at Paul's suggestion and then fell with the realization that he simply liked Frisbee throwing. He'd probably have the same response with Jas or Cal. She had hoped today would present an opportunity for the two of them to have some quality one-on-one time. Not smart, girl. He's the director. Everyone wants some of his time. He's one hundred percent absorbed with The Prayer Place and its issues. *Lord, open a door for Paul and me somehow.*

"How about I bring you a plate of fresh grilled brats, slaw, baked beans, and potato salad in a few minutes?"

"Brats! You got brats girl? They're my favorite."

She blushed again. "That's what I heard. They should be good ones. Julius said he'd get the meat at a local German meat market. They should be able to make them right."

"I can't wait. I'm salivating already. Give me a brat and I'll follow you anywhere." Paul joked.

If only it were that simple. "My pleasure, mister director. By the way, can you save me a seat? I have a couple of things I want to discuss with you."

Paul's eyebrows rose in apparent surprise. "Good things I hope."

"Of course, a few ideas I've been thinking about for improvements."

"Wow. Brats, beans, and better ideas from mission control. You throw a great party, Mary Poppins."

"Mary Poppins?"

"Oops. Yeah, that's our nickname for you. Didn't you know that? It's a compliment—your cheery nature, good looks, and you sing like Julie Andrews."

Mary covered her face with her hands. "Oh no. I had no idea. How did you know I like to sing?"

"Duh, we hear you. You sing around the store sometimes."

"Oh my goodness. I didn't realize I was so loud. I'll stop."

Jas spoke up, "No, don't stop. We like it. It's nice, especially when we're dealing with difficult customers."

Cal said, "Hey, how about a Prayer Place choir? I bet there're some good singers in the Fresh Fire folks."

Mary held up her hand like a cop stopping traffic. "Ok, people. Mary Poppins says it's time for lunch. This conversation is entirely out of hand."

She looked around. "By the way, Paul, I invited Pastor Oates and his wife. I hope that's okay." She pointed to a car pulling in. "Here they are now."

"Okay? Sure—another brilliant idea from our own Mary."

They both strode over to greet them. "Pastor Sandy, welcome. Mary told me she invited you and Kay. I'm most surprised, and so glad you came."

"Paul, I've heard so many good things about you and The Prayer Place that you couldn't keep me away. I'm sure I'd have crashed the party if Mary hadn't invited us."

Paul's cheeks flushed. "Thank you, Pastor. I assume you know the Fresh Fire folks here, and Mary. Have you met Jas and Cal, part of our team from Branham?"

After introductions and handshakes, Sandy said, "Paul, you'll never guess who visited me the other day."

"Does Mary know?" Paul asked, smiling at her. "She seems to know everything."

"I don't think so. Professor Henning and Dean Schneider. We had a good discussion, and I'm sure we'll have more. They want to keep your project going."

"Yes, they told us. So, did you talk about anything in particular?"

"Oh, money and who would manage it. No decisions yet." He paused and appeared to be thinking. "He also mentioned that he talked to your dad. I hope he can cut a deal with mall management."

"Cool," Paul said. "How much would all that cost? And how would we pay for it? Donations? Are we getting much, Mary?"

She waved her arm at the food-laden table. "That's how we funded this picnic. I didn't need to ask for donations. In fact, I wanted to talk with you about our own credit card processing. Some of our guests have asked if we take them. They want to donate, but don't carry a lot of cash or their check books."

Paul frowned, "We want no appearance of suggesting that people pay for prayer."

Mary gave him a condescending glance. "Of course not. This is coming from the guests, not us. Many of them are extremely appreciative. And, I guess, being starving students doesn't hurt either." She turned to the table, then turned back, "And I mean that literally."

She spoke in a loud voice to the whole group. "Listen up people. Here's the drill: find your seat, take your plate to Julius at the grill to get your meat, and any buns or bread you want with it, and condiments. Then get a seat at the table and we do the rest family style."

They all laughed and followed her directions. Mary saw Pastor Oates and Kay take seats opposite her and Paul. *There goes any chance for Paul and me to talk in private. Later, Lord?*

***

Pastor Oates said, "Mary, this is a wonderful picnic. I want you in my church to organize ours." He laughed, accompanied by others. "And, to make our contribution to this party, we brought something for any of you with a sweet tooth." He walked to the trunk of his car, returning with a large sheet cake. It said, 'Congratulations and God bless The Prayer Place.' That bought a round of claps, whistles and cheers.

Mary covered her mouth in shock. "Oh my. That's beautiful. Thank you so much. I had no idea." She looked around. "I'll have to find something to serve it on."

Kay Oates stepped up with a bag of paper plates, plastic forks, and a cake server. "Here you are, Mary. This might help. Our spies said there would be about twenty-five people here. So that's what I planned for."

"Oh my goodness, oh my goodness, oh my goodness." Mary said, still in shock with tears in her eyes. She spotted Paul watching her reaction. "We all thank you so much."

Paul added, "We sure do. This is great." He took a generous helping of cake. "Now we're going to have to get some exercise to work this off." He stood up, then sat down again and spoke to Mary. "How about I organize everyone cleaning up their own mess?"

She tuned to him and held his arm. "That'd be wonderful, Paul." She tried to look in his eyes, but he was already trying to locate the trash barrel. "Your turn to delegate." She smiled. He smiled back, with that boyish grin she loved. She resisted the urge to run her hands through his curly auburn hair. Will that time come? She felt her pulse pick up again, her hands moist with perspiration. "Paul, is your offer to teach me to Frisbee still open?"

Paul frowned a moment, then appeared to brighten up. This time he looked in her eyes. "Sure. Let's get this cleaned up first. And you said you had ideas about improvements."

Mary regretted mentioning them now. She wanted to focus on him, not The Prayer Place. "Ah, yeah, but they can wait. This will be more fun–right?"

"Okay, my discs are in my trunk." He returned with a cylindrical zip bag, which he opened to reveal a stack of throwing discs of all colors and styles. "This will be great. I haven't had a chance to throw since we came to town."

Mary said, "My, such a lot of them. What are they all for?"

Paul smiled, "Yeah, I guess I've picked up quite a few over the years. They are like golf clubs. You know, drivers, putters, chip shots. And," he cleared his throat, "And loaners, for people who haven't got one of their own. Would you like to pick one? Why don't we start by playing catch?"

She reached for a dark aqua disc. "This is pretty."

Paul restrained her wrist, "Um, how about we get one that's easier to see in the brush for starters? We don't want to spend all our time looking for it." He pulled out a bright yellow one. "How's this?"

She let her arm linger in his grip. "It's fine. Lead on."

Paul stood up and looked at her. "Okay," he seemed a bit nervous. "Let's start with the throw. There are two styles, backhand and forehand."

***

Within a few minutes they were playing catch at a few yards apart. "Now," Paul said, "Let's stretch it out." He walked back about fifty feet and sailed a gentle toss straight to her. "Good catch!"

Mary took a firm grip on her disc, stepped into her throw, and careened it off into the bushes behind Paul. He clapped, "Wow, you've got some power. I hope you watched where it went."

She hadn't, but no way would she admit that. After all, he didn't tell her to. "I think so. I guess now we look for it. I can see why you suggested a yellow one."

As they strode to the far side of the field together she cleared her throat and said, "So, Paul, what happens after you get your Master's? That's next spring, right?"

He looked surprised and stopped walking. His boyish grin slipped out again. "Yeah. Ah, I guess I get a job. Dr. Henning talked a little about a doctorate, but I'm not that academic. School's fine, but it will be time to go to work."

"Do you know what you want to do?"

"Not really. I assumed it would be on a church staff some place, but to tell the truth, this Prayer Place experience is having a major effect me. So I now I'm not sure what it will be.

"Ah, do you see anything else besides a job?"

"Like what?"

"Oh, you know, like a wife, kids, a family."

The grin broke out full force, crinkling his dimples. "Well, yeah," he paused, "Sure. How about you? What are your answers to your questions?"

"My answer is that I would like to find my Frisbee." She forced a laugh. "I'll plan my life a little later."

He raised an eyebrow. "Okay, Mary Poppins, works for me. Where do you think we should look?"

She stepped close to him. "Paul, I'm not sure. Didn't it go over these bushes somewhere in here?" She motioned over his shoulder, brushing his body in the process.

Paul glanced back toward the picnic area.

"What are you looking for?"

He turned to her and pulled her close to him. "To confirm we have some privacy."

"What for?"

"This," he said as their lips met.

Chapter 26

Cal held the mall door open for his colleagues. "You all up for pizza tonight? How about Cicero's?"

"Sounds good," Jas replied. "Be there in a few minutes. I'm hungry. We've had a long day."

Leave it to Cal to think of food. "Me too," Mary said. "Yes, we're tired, but you guys were great. It looked to me like God answered almost all of your prayers. And we set a record for mothers with little kids today. Even some babies. But they were all well-behaved." She pointed out into the parking lot. "Oh-oh. The light's out where we parked. Couldn't know that this morning."

Paul said, "Where's your car?"

She pointed. "Over there. A little beyond that burned out light." She glanced around. "We should be okay."

"Want us to walk you over? It's pretty dark over there. You know Jerry told us to watch out for gangs."

"Nah. I don't see anybody. Do you?"

He surveyed the lot. "I guess not. Okay, fine, meet you at Cicero's."

***

"Well, well, well. What do we have here? Blade pointed out the windshield as he coasted to a quiet stop and flicked off his lights. Two of the honeys from that Prayer

Place. I wonder where that gorilla is that they had to protect them the first time?"

His passengers crowded together in the back seat to get a better view. "Hey, cool," Spade said. "What are you going to do?"

"Let's sit here a moment. They must have a car out here. Maybe they need a little male protection, shall we say— and companionship?" They all smiled as they watched.

A voice from the back said, "Do you think ..." He stopped talking as the girls hustled toward the dark corner of the lot. "Hot, damn! Man, they're parked over by that dead light."

Blade slipped back into drive and eased closer to the edge of the lot.

"Hey, where are you going?" another voice demanded from the back.

"I'm making an end run, stupid. We'll come in from their blind side. Nice and quiet like." He turned around to face the speaker, an anorexic-looking fifteen-year-old. "That okay with you, Skinny?"

Skinny jerked back in his seat. "Yeah, sure, that's fine Blade. Smart." His knee pumped up and down and he bit his lip. "What, ah, what are we going to do with them?"

Blade smiled, "Oh, we'll find out. We only want to be friendly. Right guys? Friendly and appreciated for our finer qualities."

Spade chuckled. "Oh-huh. 'Finer qualities.' I like that. You're a real word smith Blade."

"So Spade, you stand next to the driver's door, and Skinny, cover the passenger side. Can you do that?"

"Sure, Blade. Sure I can." A weak voice came from the back seat.

"No sign of the big guy?" Blade asked.

A chorus replied, "No!"

"Okay, game time." He stopped and opened his door with care to minimize the sound.

***

Mary grabbed Jas's arm to slow her down. "Oh-oh. Here comes trouble," she said as the five youths came around her car.

The tall one with the do-rag started toward them. "Hi girls. Nice to see you out this evening."

"You leave us alone. We don't want any trouble," Jas said. "We just want to go home."

"Hey, I can dig that. But all alone? That's no fun. We can show you a real good time." He reached for her shoulder.

"Hey! Don't touch me, creep." Jas batted his hand away and bumped into someone as she stepped back. One of the boys had slipped around behind them and grabbed her waist with both hands. She wrenched herself free and stepped sideways.

"Creep? That's not respectful. I'm Deshawn, but most people call me Blade. Can you guess why?" He pulled out a switchblade, flicked it open and waved the four-inch blade in front of her face. "So what's your name, sweet cheeks?"

Mary grabbed his arm and tried to twist it. "You stop that!"

Blade jerked his knife arm up. "Chill, girl. We don't want no one to get hurt, do we? We're here to show you an enjoyable time." He closed the knife blade, but kept it in his hand.

Mary elbowed Jas and screamed, "Help, help us!" She waved at some car lights. "Help. Over here, over here." The lights swerved in their direction. "Thank you, Jesus," she sighed.

The car stopped a few feet from the group. Both doors opened in unison as Paul and Cal jumped out. "Hey, you guys. Get out of here! Go on, go home!" Paul commanded.

Blade stepped forward grinning. "Oh? You two gonna' make us? You be two, we be five."

Paul smiled. "Oh, we're not alone. I brought my Italian friend, too."

Blade frowned. "Dat so? I don't see nobody, Cracker."

"Right here," Paul said as he racked a shell into the firing chamber of a semi-automatic pistol.

"I'd like you to meet Mr. Beretta and his nine millimeter friends."

Chapter 27

"Excuse me. Is Loretta here this afternoon?" Sybil asked.

Mary looked up, smiled. *Oh my, the witches are back.* "She's due in at three, although she often gets here early. Do you want to talk to her? Have her pray for you?"

Sybil glanced behind her as Vestal came through the door. She whispered so low that Mary had to lean over to hear. "Maybe later."

Mary looked at her. "Then why don't you have a seat?"

They took seats in the crowded waiting area. Vestal leaned over and said in her ear. "What were you and that girl talking about?"

"Oh, I wondered if that lady I talked to last time was coming in. She was real nice, and I wanted to ask her about some things she said."

Vestal hissed, "Well, don't forget why we're here, girl."

Sybil turned to her. "Vestal, we may be on separate pages for some of this. If I want to talk to one of their people, you know what? I will."

Vestal sat up abruptly and turned her attention to the other people. Mothers with very young children flanked them. The baby in the stroller on her right looked at her, her lower lip quivered. Soon she whimpered. Her mother offered her a pacifier which the baby wanted no part of it and cried. Her mother picked her up, rocked her, and talked to her in a low, soothing voice. She was not to be consoled. But when the mother took her out to the mall corridor, the baby relaxed right away and drifted off to sleep. The mother returned to place her in her stroller with care without waking her.

The baby on the left looked up and smiled at Sybil, who smiled back. Sybil asked the mother, "What, three, four months?"

"Actually, six. He was a preemie." She sighed. "Praise God, he's doing okay now. It was touch and go at the beginning."

"What's his name?"

"Carlton. Charlie for short."

Sybil leaned down to the baby carrier, "Hi Charlie," she said as she fingered his little hand, "How are you? Are you a good boy?"

Charlie cooed, and smiled at her.

"He's a wonderful boy. We call him our miracle baby. I had such a hard time getting pregnant. We even tried in vitro fertilization–twice. Cost a small fortune and didn't work. We'd conceive, carry for a few weeks, and stop. So when we finally looked at adoption—viola a baby! And he smiles now. We love it." She turned to Sybil. "Hi, I'm Rachel. Pardon my asking, but I couldn't help looking. Are you expecting?"

"Yes, yes I am. I guess I show now. I'm Sybil by the way." She felt a dig in her ribs from Vestal. "What?"

The baby's eyes shifted to Vestal and he let out a scream, almost as if in pain. Vestal glared at him. She said, "See what you did, Sybil, you scared him."

Rachel picked him up, turned him away from the two witches, and comforted him. He quieted down. She spoke in a low, gentle voice, "To be honest, ma'am, I'd say it was you, not Sybil. He's afraid of you for some reason."

"Because I look different—albino?" Vestal demanded.

Rachel blushed and frowned, then raised an eyebrow. "It's hard to say what a baby perceives, but I guarantee he's never seen anything like Sybil's studs and Goth makeup before, and he seems to like her."

"Well, I refuse to be judged by an infant." Vestal proclaimed as she stood up. "Come on Sybil."

Sybil didn't budge. "I, ah, I'm going to stay here for a while. I still want to talk to Loretta."

"Loretta is it? Now you call her by name? Okay, you call me when you get out of here. You got that, girl?"

"We'll see." Sybil looked at her, stone faced.

After a few moments Rachel said, "She didn't seem like a very happy person."

"I never thought of it that way, but you're right, she's not. I guess she's had a lot of abuse in her life, abuse and loneliness."

"Too bad. A far too common story"

"Yeah, in fact, it's mine too. That's what Vestal and I have in common."

"I'm so sorry. So, Sybil, is this your first child?"

She wants to change the subject, but has no idea this new one is a minefield. How do I answer her? Tell her I sacrificed my baby to Molech? Sybil pursed her lips, then said low, "No, it's my second. My first one didn't make it."

Rachel squeezed her arm. "Oh, I am so sorry. Please forgive me. I didn't realize."

"Oh, it's not your fault. I figured I wasn't cut out to be a mother, didn't have the right instincts. But now, now I'm not so sure."

"That's wonderful, what's changed?"

"Well, we were in here a while ago, and a lady named Loretta talked to me a little. And she had, it was like a kindness about her that touched me. She was like you, had a lot of trouble with her baby, but came through. In fact, she called it what you said about yours, a miracle baby. And then, to be honest, just today, your Charlie."

"Charlie?"

Sybil had trouble talking and reached for a tissue. "Yes, he looked at me, and he liked me, he actually liked me." She looked at Rachel. "People are not supposed to like me, not like this, not with all these rings, studs and dark makeup."

"Sybil, we all have our own stories, our own reasons for doing things. If people aren't supposed to like you, what are they supposed to do?"

She smiled. "Well, I suppose I expect them to be shocked, and maybe afraid."

"Afraid?"

"Sure. Then they won't hurt me. They'll leave me alone."

Rachel sat back and eased Charlie back in his seat. His big blue eyes stared up at both of them. "Whew. That's, that's—what can I say? Sybil, it's sad. I'm sad for you. What a way to live." She paused and frowned. "What about Jesus? What about Him? He can help." She studied Sybil's makeup shrouded eyes. "Are you familiar with Him?"

"Hah!" Sybil almost shrieked. "You start that stuff, I'm out of here."

Rachel smiled, "Oops, stepped into that one didn't I? Sorry."

A young man came around the corner and walked up to her. He reached down to Charlie. "Hi Charlie, how's my buddy? You like to talk to these good looking ladies?"

Rachel stood and hugged him, "Hi, honey. Everything go okay?"

"Sure did. Look." He flexed his hands and wrists. "No pain. God is good." His eyes met Sybil's who watched their little interchange. "Hi, I'm Tad. I'm Rachel's better half, and the father of a future President of the United States."

Sybil laughed, "Hi, Tad. I've been talking to your wife and charmed by your son. I guess now I can tell people I met a future President."

Tad laughed. "Might want to wait on that one a bit." He turned to Rachel as he picked up Charlie in his carrier. "Ready to go?"

Rachel held her hand up like a caution sign and turned to Sybil. "Sybil, how about a hug? You up for that?"

Sybil rose slowly. "I, ah, I guess so."

Rachel wrapped her arms around her and caressed her back as she hugged her. She whispered in her ear. "You are not alone. Talk to Loretta, she's wonderful."

Sybil wiped her eyes. "Thanks, Rachel, thanks a lot." She waved at Charlie. "Bye, bye Charlie." And again wiped her eyes as they left.

Loretta, turned around from speaking with Mary. "Sybil! You came back. So glad to see you. To tell you the truth, after your first visit with your friend, I figured we'd never see either of you again. Mary says you wanted to talk to me. What's going on, dear?" Her grey eyes sparkled and her white curls bounced as she talked.

Sybil cleared her throat. "I, ah, must be my hormones I reckon. I'm confused. You saw I was pregnant almost before I did. Nobody else did. And you were so kind to me before. I felt good afterword, a different kind of good than normal drugs or sex. So I wanted to talk about it, find out where you're coming from."

"That would be fine, dear." She took a clipboard from Mary's desk. "Tell you what, we have our procedures of course, so would you mind filling this out to help us learn a bit more about you? You can put something like 'discuss feelings' in the space for what you want today. And if you don't want actual prayer, but only to talk about it, that's fine too. It will also give us more privacy than out here in the waiting area."

"Okay."

***

As they eased down into the comfy chairs in the prayer room, Loretta leaned over and rested her hand on Sybil's. "You're having a hard time, aren't you, dear?"

Sybil nodded, "Yes. It's this baby thing. I didn't expect to be pregnant, have another one."

"'Another one?' This is not the first?"

"No, but that's another story. He's gone."

"I'm so sorry. Go on, dear."

"I didn't believe I was mother material, could do a good job raising a kid. But now, now I think I want this baby. I want to be a good mother." She looked at Loretta, "But I'm ignorant. I was raised in foster homes and reform school. I don't know nothing about babies. I never had a real mother. How am I going to be one? I—I'm scared!" She held her head in her hands and sobbed.

Loretta slid her chair right next to Sybil's and held her tight. Sybil's eyes streamed mascara down her cheeks and her nose ran when she looked at Loretta. "I'm sorry, I must look a mess."

"Not to me. You're beautiful. Sybil, you're a beautiful person." She wiped Sybil's face with a tissue. "Can I ask you a question?"

Sybil blinked through the tears and muttered, "Sure."

"How about God? Ever think about Him?"

Sybil frowned and shook her head. "No, not really."

"Well, let me tell you about Him. Would you like to hear what He has to say to you, you personally? Is that okay?"

"Sure, I guess."

Loretta began, pausing between each sentence.

"My child,you may not know me, but I know everything about you.

I know when you sit down and when you rise up.

I am familiar with all your ways.

Even the very hairs on your head are numbered.

For you were made in my image.

In me you live and move and have your being.
For you are my offspring.

I knew you even before you were conceived.

I chose you when I planned creation.
You were not a mistake, for all your days are written in my book."

And she continued with scripture after scripture.

Sybil wept heavily through most of it and hugged Loretta hard when she finished. "That was beautiful. Is it true?"

"Every word, yes it is true. It's all from the Bible."

They talked about many things, including Sybil's first baby. At last Sybil rose, wiped her eyes for the last time. "I guess I used a lot of your tissues."

"That's why we stock a lot. For you, and the Lord's work. Are you going to be okay now, dear?"

"Yeah, I guess. I can come back, right?"

"Of course, as often as you want." Loretta walked her out to the door. As soon as it closed she told Mary, "Get Paul. Now."

He came over moments later. "Mrs. Youngman, what's up?"

"I just had a guest confess to murdering her baby."

Chapter 28

Kamal's pulse raced as he drove while Yasir navigated. Fresh tissues hung in a bush at the last two turns. "Did you put out those tissues?"

"Yes, I wanted to be sure we could find our way today."

"What were you thinking? Now they will lead somebody right to our test site."

"Not after the rain we're predicted to get soon. They'll wash off and disappear in the mud. It will be okay, my friend."

Kamal looked at the dark sky. Yasir was probably right. "How did you find this place again?"

"I started with Google Maps. I wanted open woods, not too far from town, but away from buildings. So I scanned Google satellite until I located this area. We're in a state forest, so I figured not much habitation. You wait. I believe you'll like it. But slow down. This last turn is tricky."

Kamal stopped at a bush with a tissue. It marked a two-lane track through dense grass. "Is that where we go? I don't see any fresh tire tracks. Did you come here yesterday?"

"I did, but I walked this last part. I didn't want to get stuck in a ditch or something. But the ground's all solid, so we're safe to drive. Why don't you turn around so we can head out before we set off the bomb?"

"Good idea." He leaned forward to see the trail in front of his car as he edged their way through the thick grass. "Did you pick a spot to set it up?"

Yasir nodded and pointed ahead to the left. "How about the base of that tall tree? Does that look all right?"

Kamal rolled down his window for a better look. "Yeah, this looks okay. Let me turn the car around first before we take anything out. You're right. We don't want to get stuck back here. Can you walk ahead of me and make sure I stay on solid ground?"

"Good idea. Sure."

A few minutes later Kamal popped his trunk and hopped out. "I'll put the bomb right at the base of that tree. I'd like to see how much damage we get." He paced through the brush to a large elm tree and scraped a spot clear with his foot. Then he settled the bomb by the tree and led the fuse toward his car. "Where do you want to stand when it detonates?"

Yasir scanned the little clearing and pointed. "How about behind those trees?"

"Looks good. I'll light it and then run over and join you."

He stretched the fuse out full length and lit the end with his lighter. As he ran toward Yasir, he plunged full length onto the ground. When he sat up, he found a wire wrapped around his ankle from an old fence. "Help!" Then he rethought his cry and yelled. "No, stay there. It's too dangerous. I should be okay."

As he turned to lie down again a deafening explosion and a blinding flash hurled him to the ground. His clothes sucked in tight to his body, and then all ballooned away from him. His entire body quivered from the blast. After lying still for several minutes he gingerly rolled over and sat up again. Leaves and small branches suspended in the air floated earthward. A shattered stalk reaching up to the sky was all that remained of the elm tree, with a four foot pit in front where the bomb had been. His hand came away bright red with blood when he rubbed his nose. Blinking and screwing his eyes shut several times helped clear his vision. His muscles vibrated and twitched.

Where was Yasir? Was he okay? His friend slowly emerged from his hiding place without a sound. "Yasir!" He knew he yelled, but heard nothing. His friend's mouth moved. Again silence. "I can't hear you. I can't hear anything. I'm totally deaf!"

As he struggled to stand, a sharp pain stabbed the heel of his right foot. He plopped back on the ground and reached for his shoe. When he pushed it part way off the pain stopped. He kicked it off and examined the shoe. A jagged piece of broken pipe had pierced through the heel and sole. *Dear Allah, what if it had been a couple of inches over? That'd have sliced right through my leg. I was very, very lucky. Amazing, almost no pain.*

Yasir touched his shoulder. "Are you okay?" He examined the metal shard from Kamal's shoe. "That was a close call."

Kamal shook his head, pointed to his ears. "Nothing."

Yasir pointed to his eyes, then Kamal's jacket. Kamal slipped it off to find it riddled with small holes and tears. He wriggled his back muscles but didn't feel anything. He looked at Yasir, "I was lucky, real lucky."

Yasir shook his head in agreement, then pointed to the car and made a steering wheel sign. "We better get out of here."

Kamal tried to get up and found his other foot still wrapped in the wire that had tripped him. He pointed to it. "This may have saved my life."

Yasir nodded and helped Kamal unwind the wire. Kamal had to lean on Yasir as he limped to the car. Yasir decided not to point out all the little pings and dents the bomb had made in the trunk lid and back window. Praise Allah the tires were intact. Kamal pulled out his car keys. "You drive."

Yasir gave him a thumbs up, helped Kamal fasten his seat belt and slipped in behind the wheel.

As they neared Kamal's apartment, Kamal said, "I believe my hearing is coming back. Say something."

"Are you okay?"

"Yeah, I'm pretty sure I am. I sure didn't expect this to turn out this way. I'm done with bombs. Too dangerous."

"What are you going to do?"

"I don't know."

I do, but I won't tell you. How I get a gun in America?

Chapter 29

Pastor Wallace Strinch dressed down for his second visit to
The Prayer Place. This time he wore a taupe Polo shirt, tan
Dockers, and Rockport loafers. He smiled. "Hi, it's Mary–
right?"

She returned his smile and looked perplexed. "Pastor,
ah, Strinch? Did I remember that right?"

"You sure did. Well done. How are you this
afternoon?"

"I'm fine, Pastor. What brings you here? I suppose
you'd like to talk to Paul again.

"If I might." He signed the visitor clip board. "Is that
possible?"

She checked her computer. "It should be in a few
minutes. He's with a guest at the moment. Might I add that
next time you can call and I will reserve a time slot for you. In
the meantime, would you like to take a seat in the waiting
area?"

As he eased himself into a chair, a curly haired toddler
in a Batman tee shirt came over. "Hi, I'm Robby. What's your
name?"

Pastor Strinch shook his head in amazement at the
child's friendliness. "Hi, Robby, I'm Wally." He looked for
Robby's mother, but saw no likely candidates. He noticed a

silver-haired gentleman watching them. "Robby, is your mommy here?"

"Yeah, she's real sick. She came so Jesus can make her better." He turned and pointed to the gentleman. "That's my papaw. He helps us a lot now."

"That's nice Robby. I hope your mommy gets better."

"Lung cancer," the senior said, in a low voice. "Stage three."

"That's too bad. Serious, very serious."

Wally sat still, searching for the right thing to say.

"Mommy!" Robby shouted and ran up to her as she came around the corner. "Are you all better?"

She reached for her son. Tears streamed down her cheeks. "I'm a lot better Robby." She pulled a green oxygen bottle with tubing coiled around the regulator which she showed her son. "See, I don't need my air tube." She took a deep breath and let it out. "And I can breathe real deep again."

She turned to the older gentleman. "Dad, it was incredible. They just talked and prayed, and this wave came over me and like it washed my lungs clean. I have to go to the doctor again and get checked out, but Dad, I have hope for the first time in months." They hugged as she sobbed into his shoulder.

Wally studied her. *How can this be? Is this the devil's work?*

Paul's approach interrupted his thoughts. "Pastor Strinch, this is a surprise. Although I told one of my colleagues, you would be back."

"Did you really? Why did you say that?"

Paul looked a little self-conscious. "Well, as I recall, I said you'd be back because everything we do here violates one of your basic beliefs."

Wally frowned. "Hm, that's true. Paul, you're a wise man, especially for someone so young." He paused. "Ah, could we go someplace with a little more privacy?"

"Sure." Paul turned to Mary. "Can you see if Julius can join us? Wally, do you mind? Julius is one of our experienced volunteers with far more years of prayer for healing than I have."

"That'll be fine." Wally replied as he followed Paul into a prayer room. Julius had preceded them. "Are you Julius? I'm Pastor Wallace Strinch, but please, call me Wally."

They shook hands and sat in a circle. Wally looked at them. "So, why am I here? On the way over I rehearsed all of my theological arguments for why healing ended with the death of the last Apostle. I planned to claim my secretary's supposed healing of her bad hip was psychosomatic." He fell silent, then continued in a quiet voice. "I won't do that, for two reasons. First, it won't do a bit of good. You folks won't stop what you're doing, and shut this place down. And second, to tell the truth, now I'm not so sure. While I sat in the waiting area, a little boy talked to me about how Jesus would heal his mother. His grandfather said she had stage three lung cancer. But this young fellow's faith was so simple, so pure, it reminded me of the scripture, 'unless you are converted and become as little children, you will by no means enter the Kingdom of Heaven.' Matthew 18 as I recall."

Paul and Julius listened intently. "And?" Paul said.

"And I realized I lost that simple faith a long, long time ago—probably in seminary. Simple faith was not encouraged." He bit his lip. "Then this kid's mother came out from prayer, dragging her oxygen bottle, which she no longer needed. She took a deep breath to show her son how Jesus healed her." He looked at them both. "I've known a few stage three lung cancer patients. They can't do that." He paused again. "So I don't know what to think."

Julius signaled Paul that he wanted to intervene. "Wally, may I ask you a question?"

"Sure." Wally looked surprised.

"I'm picking up pain coming from you, physical pain—not the emotional distress of questioning your core beliefs. It seems to be coming from your feet. So Wally, do your feet hurt? Your toes?"

Wally sat back in his chair. "That's amazing! Yes, I have hammer toes, bad ones. They hurt a lot."

"What are hammer toes?" Paul asked. "I never heard of them."

"Here. I'll show you," He kicked off one of his loafers and stripped off his sock to reveal bent and deformed toes, red and swollen. "Not a pretty sight. And, yes, I wear the right kind of shoes. These loafers are not nearly as tight as my dress oxfords."

Julius spoke. "Question two Wally. May I pray for them?" He looked at Wally for an answer.

Wally smiled, "I, ah, I guess so. Sure. After all this, I say okay. Go for it." He kicked off his other shoe and pulled off the second sock. "Might as well do them both. They need it." He seemed to draw himself up as if preparing for an ordeal.

"Wally, you don't have to do a thing, just receive." Julius explained. "If you don't mind I'll apply a little anointing oil. You know the scripture in James 5:14 'Is anyone among you sick? Let him call for the elders of the church, and let them pray over him, anointing him with oil in the name of the Lord.'' Wally nodded. "And what does it say next? I paraphrase. 'They will be healed.' Not 'might be' but 'will be'. Julius pulled a small vial out of his pocket and unscrewed the cap. "I love the scent of this, frankincense in olive oil from Jerusalem." He held it out for Wally to sniff.

Julius dabbed a little on his finger and touched each of Wally's hammer toes.

Paul asked, "Can I put my hand on your head?

"Sure. Whatever you want to do."

Wally closed his eyes as they prayed, and his shoulders dropped as his body relaxed. He wriggled his fingers and smiled. Then he wiggled his toes. The more he flexed the straighter they became. He let out an audible sigh. "I can feel it, feel it working." He opened his eyes and studied his feet. "Oh my God. Thank you Jesus." He looked at Paul and Julius, "There's no pain. It's gone." A tear welled up in his eye and ran down his cheek. "I don't believe it. But I *do* believe it."

He grabbed their hands. "I was wrong. He does heal today. This is not the work of the devil. It's the Holy Spirit." He turned to Paul. "Paul, forgive me for the horrible way I treated you on my last visit."

Paul squeezed his hand. "No problem. You are forgiven—by me at least. You have to forgive yourself too. That may be harder."

Wally shook his head, "Yes, it may. I'm not known as a very forgiving guy. I guess that'll need to change."

Paul stood up. "Wally, we've covered a lot of ground today, made some real progress. Looking ahead, you'll have to come to terms with your old self—and your denomination. We'd be happy to pray for you again, for the Lord's leading as you chart your course from here. But we are not a counseling service. You might want to consult with my pastor, Sandy Oates, about it. I know he'll be quite receptive."

Wally stood too and shook his head. "Yeah, I can't start banging on the pulpit and preaching a whole new theology out of the blue.' He shook his head sideways several times. "I need to pray and let this settle." He shook hands with them again, "Thank you gentlemen, thank you so much. I will go now. My wife won't believe it."

After he left, Julius leaned over and asked Paul. "So, great prophet, will he return?"

"My money says 'yes.'"

"Really? What for?"

"To find out how to do this himself."

Chapter 30

Mary sat erect in bed. *What was that? It seemed so real—must have been a God dream.* She remembered at school last winter some guy prophesied over her. He said she should record her dreams. God would communicate with her. She hadn't done it. She didn't want to give up her usual entrance into the waking world every morning—a gradual and reluctant process, while her dreams faded into the distant past as she regained full consciousness. Not this time. She was wide awake, all at once.

She pushed off the covers, shuffled over to her desk, and searched for a clean piece of paper. Aha, found one. She wrote down the precise words, then reread it. It looked like a letter to Paul, a letter of warning. Should she call him? No. Who knew when or how he got up? If his mornings resembled hers, he'd at least want his coffee, and maybe even a full breakfast before he tackled a new issue. But a text could work. He'd get it in his time, not hers.

She sent, "Paul, need to talk first thing. Had a very disturbing dream about The Prayer Place. A warning." How to sign it? Not 'Love', not 'Fondly'. 'Yours' would work. She typed, 'Yours, Mary.' And punched send.

Okay, girl, time to get ready for the real world. But keep an eye on the phone in case he answers. Jas sat at the breakfast table when she skipped downstairs. Oh-oh. Running late already.

"Morning, Mary, are you okay? You look kind of flustered."

"Had a God dream. 'We will be tested. Soon'."

"What?" Jas sounded very skeptical.

"First, let me eat. I can explain in the car."

***

The two girls arrived at the service entrance to The Prayer Place as Paul unlocked the door. He touched her arm. "Okay, Mary, what's this big dream you texted me about? The God dream?"

"Paul, do you remember when Esra Muldoon came to chapel last fall and told me to record my dreams?"

"I don't recall the dream part about you, but I do remember he said God communicated in dreams today as he did in Biblical times. Is that what happened?"

Mary blushed. "Yes I'd say it did." She turned to face him and took his arm. "Paul, it was so real. I've never had a dream like this."

"Okay, okay. Chill, girl. What did God say?"

"Well, it wasn't like a phone call from God. But the message was, 'Beware, a test will come in the next few days. Someone will try to trick you.'"

"Trick me?" Paul asked. "Do you mean me, personally?"

"No, no. I'm sure the message meant The Prayer Place."

"Did they say what kind of trick?"

Mary took a deep breath. "For some reason, I think it's about us giving medical advice." She looked in his eyes. "Why? Would that be a trick?"

Paul smiled. "Could be. The enemy wants us to do that. If we give somebody medical advice or opinions, they could sue us for practicing medicine without a license. Even if it's not true, we wouldn't survive a lawsuit for anything." He stepped back and held his fist up to his lips.

Hm, must need to think.

He smiled, put his hand on her shoulder, and said, "First, thank you for being alert to this and telling me right away. I hope everyone here knows we never give medical advice or suggestions to our guests even if it's from our personal experience. But I'll put together a short reminder of that, and alert people to pay attention when someone seems to solicit it. Can you text it to the whole staff?"

"Not quite. We've got two or three people who can't or don't get text messages. I'll print off hard copies for them and have a few to spare." She closed her eyes and said, "God, you are so good. You know everything, and you have warned us. Now it's up to us to pay heed."

"Amen," Paul said. "We'll make you the unofficial Prayer Place chaplain, Mary."

Mary's cheeks turned pink, and she shook her head. "I'm here to help. That's all. That little prayer just came to me."

"It's obvious that your spiritual sensitivity is on the upswing. Well done, Mary Poppins."

***

A few days later Emma Ratliff checked her reflection in a store window. Tousled hair, no make-up except misapplied lipstick, an old dress, worn tennis shoes over sagging socks, and a canvas bag for a purse. Good—the right image. She verified that she'd switched on her wire, looked in the door of The Prayer Place, and pushed it in. Although she knew exactly what she was doing, she acted confused and shambled over to the girl at the desk.

Mary looked up, frowned, then smiled. "Hi. I'm Mary. Are you here for prayer?"

Emma studied her fresh, eager face. *These kids have no idea what they're doing.* "I, ah, I guess so. I need some help here. I'm so confused. I feel rotten. What can I do? Can you help me?"

Mary reached out and touched her hand. "I don't myself, but we have people here that will pray for you. We'll get you a prayer team soon." She handed Emma a clipboard. "Would you sit over there and fill this out?"

I guess I need to do this to get in the door. Let's see, who shall I be today? How about Susan Greenlee? She wrote that in the space for her name, along with a fictitious address and church affiliation. When she got to the space that asked, 'What would you like prayer for today?' She wrote "Help!" and returned the form to the desk. *Okay, I'm Susan, the new me. Show time.*

***

"Thanks." She checked the form. "Susan. I will have Jas and Loretta with you right away." She walked in the back, found Jas sat in the break area with a cup of coffee, and handed her the form, "Got a new one, Jas. My gut says to be alert."

Jas looked up. "Okay. I'll tell Loretta. On duty." And she gave a little salute. Then she walked to the waiting area. "Susan?"

Emma started, stood up, and ambled over to Jas. She looked around at everything as Jas led her to a little room.

As they sat down, Jas introduced herself and Loretta, and held up her form. "You say 'Help!' here. That's a new one. What's going on?"

Emma wrung her hands. "Oh everything. I don't know what to do. I feel lousy, no energy, often have trouble getting my breath. My heart pounds like a jackhammer. I can't sleep, lost my job. Don't have no money—and nobody to talk to. What should I do?"

Jas and Loretta looked at each other. As Loretta spoke Emma cut her off. "Should I go to the doctor? I don't know what doctor. Do you have a doctor? What's his name? Would he see me?"

Loretta smiled, "Susan, let's try to break this down into manageable chunks. I ..."

"Oh Loretta," She wiped her eyes, "I take Tylenol for the pain, but it still hurts. Would Advil be better? Or Aleve? Or even aspirin? What do you think I should do?"

"Susan, we are a prayer place, not a medical clinic. I'm sorry but we don't give medical advice. We're not trained or certified for that."

"I see, but what about a doctor? Do you guys have a doctor, right? Where should I go?"

Jas spoke in a firm, commanding voice. "Susan, are you really here for prayer? Do you want Jesus to help you?"

Emma stood and placed her hands on her hips. "I—."

"Who do you work for? Who sent you to do this?" Jas demanded.

Loretta stared at Jas, eyes wide open. "Jas?"

Emma/Susan almost ran out the door.

Jas smiled at Loretta. "That lady was as phony as a three-dollar bill. We need to tell Paul. Mary heard from God."

Chapter 31

"Dr. Majoros, Eddie French is here."

"Thank you, Terry. Are his labs ready?" *This won't be pleasant.*

"Almost. It will be a few minutes."

"Okay, bring them in when they're ready and give me about five minutes."

"Oh, trust me, you'll want to see him." Terry looked so happy as if she were ready to dance. *What on Earth? She knows something.*

"Oh? Okay. Send him in." She giggled as she let the door swing shut.

He leaned back in his high-backed leather chair and adjusted his blue birthday present tie. Eddie had cancelled his earlier appointment, so something must have changed. It couldn't be for the good.

The door swung wide open and Eddie bounded in. "Hi, Doc! How ya' doing?" He stood beaming in the middle of the office.

Astounding. He looks almost well. "I, I'm fine, Eddie. I'd ask how you're doing but it's obvious. You look fantastic. What happened?"

Eddie extended his arms and turned in a full circle. "Jesus Christ is what happened." He pulled up a chair next to the Doctor's desk. "Doc, do you remember when I asked if you believed in prayer?"

He nodded. "Yes, I do. You mentioned a place in the mall as I recall."

"Yeah, The Prayer Place. Anyway, I went three times. The first two times I felt better—like at peace and stuff, but not my body. But this last time." He paused. "How do I say this? I guess, I guess it was like God showed up. Like He swept through my body and took out the cancer. I was amazed." He stood up and spun in a circle. "I mean, look at me. I'm almost back to my old self."

Terry came in with a copy of Eddie's lab work. She smiled at Eddie and patted his shoulder as she left.

"Thank you, Terry." Dr. Majoros said. He scanned the reports. "This confirms it. Urine is clear. Bilirubin is down. So is PSA. Your counts are close to normal, far better than they've been in months. In fact, I'd say they're the best I've ever seen from you." He reached out and shook Eddie's hand.

"Congratulations, young man. This is miraculous" He frowned a bit and said. "But as you say, you're almost back to normal, but not quite. I'd like to continue the Degarelix for a few more weeks to be sure."

Eddie sighed. "Doc, I hate that stuff. The side-effects are brutal. I get night sweats, chills, my joints ache like mad, and I still wear out if I do much of anything." He stopped talking and shook his head. "I say 'no', Doc. To be honest, I've kind of slacked off on it since my last prayer time. Tell you what, I'll go back for more prayer. They invited me to come as much as I want anyway. How does that sound?"

The doctor grinned and held up a finger. "Eddie, that sounds fine. I'll agree on one condition."

Eddie raised his eyebrows. "What's that?"

"That I come with you. I want to see what this miracle place is all about. It should be good for all my patients, right?"

"What? You want to come with me?" He shook his head. "Okay, I suppose. I bet this never happened before."

"Would they object?"

"Nah, I wouldn't think so. Why would they?" He pursed his lips, "I guess you'll want to meet Paul, their director."

"Excellent idea. Yes, I'd love to."

"Okay, give me a date and I'll call Mary and set it up."

"Terry will give you a call on that."

Eddie smiled and raised an eyebrow. "Ah, Doc, do you know if she has a boyfriend?"

Chapter 32

Mary smoothed her black dress and glanced at her reflection in the mirror. Yes, her knit dress fit well, just a hint of cleavage, and not too short. But did these black pumps have a high enough heel to slenderize her calves? This outfit would have to work. She snapped on her pearl earrings and clipped on her necklace. She spun on her heel, then slipped into the family room. With luck, no one would notice.

Oh-oh, Jas spotted her. "Hey girl, you clean up real good. You look wonderful. Big plans tonight?" Jas motioned for her to spin around, which she did, releasing a slight scent of *L'air du Temp*. "Mm-mm that smells good. My, my, you look fine."

Mary blushed. "Is it too much?"

"No way, baby-doll. So what's the big occasion? Is the President coming?"

Her twelve-year-old brother, Kevin, sang, "Mary's got a boyfriend, Mary's got a boyfriend."

Mary turned redder, "You hush up, Kevin. Mind your manners."

"Is this Paul?" Jas asked, eyebrow arched.

Mary grinned and nodded. "He asked me to dinner. Said he wants to talk about some things."

Jas pressed her hand to her mouth. "Oh my, this could be serious. Do you have any idea what he's got in mind?" She smirked. "I guess you might have a few things to discuss yourself, eh?"

"Yeah. Well, we'll see."

"Where are you going? Did he say?"

"Broadwell's, on the river." She glanced put the window. "Is that a nice place? I'm not familiar with this city."

"Nice? It's the best." Kevin proclaimed. "That's where Josh Cohen had his Bar Mitzvah. Classy, very classy, Sis."

Jas stood, tugged Mary closer to the light, and examined her makeup.

"Did I miss something? Is my lipstick smeared? I almost never wear it. Did I overdo?

Jas laughed and patted her arm. "Chill, girl. It's perfect. You're gorgeous. If he doesn't get on his knee and propose as soon as he sees you I'll want to know why."

"Jas! Not you too." She bit her lip. "Okay, I admit, I'm almost twenty-three, I graduate next spring. And I don't want to be an old maid missionary, or live in trees all my life like that British chimpanzee lady."

The doorbell chimed. Jas and Kevin exchanged grins. Jas poked. "Show time, girl."

Mary swung the front door wide open and looked Paul over from head to toe. *Wow. He's gone all out. Where did his dark blue blazer, light blue shirt, tan slacks, and shiny black shoes come from? Were they all new?* She'd never seen them before. Paul stood there, eyes agape. She gasped as he looked deep into her brown eyes.

"Mary, you look awesome."

She beamed. "Thanks, Paul. You look nice too. I decided I'd clean up a little for you. This is our first date isn't it?"

"Are you kidding? For sure. The first of many, I hope." He stepped in and reached for her hand. "Already I feel bad. I should have brought flowers. You're absolutely stunning."

She took his hand in both of hers. "Oh that's not necessary. But it's a sweet idea."

"Are you ready?"

"Sure am. Let me get a sweater—in case we want to go for a walk later."

"Good idea. This way fair lady." He settled his hand on the small of her back and guided her to a silver Jaguar XJ at the curb.

"What's this?" Mary asked. She stroked the fender and patted the door handle.

"Our ride for the evening. Is it okay?"

"If you insist." She grinned. "Is it yours?"

Paul laughed. "Not hardly. It's only for the evening with guarantees that it'll return to our garage in the exact same condition as you see it now. My dad treats it like a pet."

She loved his hand on her back and didn't want to lose it as he helped her slip into the low seat. "It's gorgeous."

"A gorgeous car for a gorgeous lady."

***

Paul smiled with relief as the Maître-d' escorted them to the table he'd reserved overlooking the river. Mary slid onto the chair Paul held for her. "This is so special. You've thought of everything. Thank you so much."

"Mary, you're the inspiration." He cleared his throat. "May I ask you a question?"

"This sounds serious. Sure, what is it?"

"How come you asked to be part of this project?"

Mary's face burned. "Perhaps I shouldn't say this, but that's easy—you."

"Me?"

She looked at him through tear-filled eyes. "Oh Paul, you can be so naïve sometimes. Yes, you. I wanted to be part of something with you, and it didn't much matter what."

He reached for her hand, and she covered it with hers. "Wow. I had no idea—of course. That's what you've been telling me. How long has this been going on?"

She looked down and spoke in a low voice. "It began in freshman orientation."

"What?"

She nodded.

"I don't know what to say, Mary. I guess I wasn't very aware of things in those days. I hope I didn't ignore you. If I did, I'm so sorry."

"That's okay. Not ignored exactly, more like just not part of your picture." As she paused a slight frown crossed her forehead. "But I don't think any girls were in your picture then."

"That's probably true. I'm told I tend to be intense, goal oriented."

She smiled and nodded but remained silent.

"Okay, a serious female relationship was not on my radar screen—then. To be honest, it hasn't been now either, until, ah, until you entered the picture."

"And you say it's changed now? You are... how did you put it? That a 'serious female relationship' *is* on your radar screen?"

Paul jerked in an irregular breath. Was he afraid to acknowledge how he felt? He searched her face and peered deep into her gold-flecked brown eyes. He squeezed her hand. "Yes, Mary. I wasn't ready for this. It wasn't in my plan. But here it is, and I know it." He rose up, drew her across the table to kiss her—and knocked over a water glass. "Oh no!" He jumped up and grabbed a napkin to blot it up, laughing at his clumsiness.

She joined his giggles and glanced around. "Please tell me nobody saw this—that nobody here knows us."

He glanced up to see two waiters standing nearby with fresh napkins. "Oops, Sorry gentlemen. I guess you still think we came for dinner. We, ah, got a little, ah, shall I say 'sidetracked'." He whispered, "I've never been so embarrassed in my life." As he sat down again.

***

Mary folded her napkin and placed it next to her plate. "That was delicious. This is a wonderful place. Thank you so much."

"Hey, you're welcome. I'm glad you liked it. At least we made it through dinner with no more mishaps. So, it's your first time here?"

"Yes. Remember my family moved here from Lafayette a year before I started at Branham. So I'm not very familiar with the town. I guess you grew up here?"

"I did. My folks wanted us kids to have a stable upbringing. My mother was an Army brat and my father's father worked as a salesman and changed jobs a lot. So, neither of them lived anywhere very long, and they both wanted better for us. They picked our house based on the school system. I guess that's what I want too."

She nodded. "Good idea."

"For sure. And now, dear lady, might I suggest an evening stroll along the river? Are you familiar with the path there?"

"No, but it sounds great."

His eyes twinkled in the dim evening light. "Some say it's romantic." He took her hand.

They strolled for several minutes, enjoying the evening air, the boats' lights passing them by, and the buildings' twinkle on the other shore. "This is all so perfect, Paul. Magical."

He turned to face her, a smile curled up his lips, "Yes, you are, Mary." He gave her a long, intimate embrace, then relaxed a bit, but didn't let go. She settled back in his arms and looked in his eyes. He said, "I have to tell you my head is spinning. This has already been an incredible summer with The Prayer Place so successful and blessed, and now this— you. I, ah, I am not super-experienced in relating to girls. I mean, I dated in high school and a little on campus, but it wasn't serious. We had fun and stayed out of trouble. Mostly we hung out together."

Mary frowned. "I see, but why are you telling me this?" *Is there something wrong with you?*

"Simply that I'd like you to be patient with me. As I proved in the restaurant, I bumble sometimes."

He held her tight again in a long, passionate kiss. She first stiffened, then melted into his arms. Her fingers ran through his auburn curls as she returned his kiss and hugged him tighter. She whispered in his ear, "Oh Paul, I've wanted to do this for four years."

He leaned back to study her. "Do what? Kiss me? We already kissed at the picnic."

She smiled lovingly. "Well, that too, but no. I meant run my fingers through your hair. That's what I first spotted when we came on campus."

"My hair? I had no idea." He stopped. "Hm, I seem to repeat that this evening." She pulled him down to her lips. "I'll be patient with you for the rest of my life. I love you, Paul." She didn't give him the chance to respond but held him in a soft, lingering kiss. At last she eased back and searched his eyes.

"And I love you." They hugged and kissed again.

His cell phone chimed. A text read: "URGENT, CALL ASAP. DAD"

"Oh-oh, Mary, what lousy timing."

"You have to call. But please, I'm here for you, let me support you."

He started punching his cell phone. "For sure. "What ever it is, I'm so glad you're here with me." He waited a moment, "Hi Dad, what's up?

"Mall security called. Somebody broke into The Prayer Place."

Chapter 33

Kamal knocked on his uncle's door. "Uncle Ahmed. S*allam alaikum.*" He bowed as the door swung open.

He gagged and stepped in. Uncle Ahmed reeked of cigars as usual and wore the same tee shirt he had on at Kamal's last visit weeks ago. Who knows when he last showered.

"Kamal! W*a-alaikum-salaam,* and peace be with you. How nice you come." He let Kamal come in, then stood back to study him. "So, how is my favorite nephew? You look— what do you look? Not face of happiness. So you limp? You do not still make bombs do you?"

"No, no, Uncle. No bombs. Not anymore."

"Anymore? What you mean? Did you try one?" He studied Kamal's expression. "You did! After I told you 'no.'" He lumbered back and forth, wringing his hands. "Kamal, I told you. Bombs are dangerous. You got hurt. That's why you limp. Did it hurt your ears? Do you have bad dreams?"

Kamal hung his head and nodded. "Yes, uncle, all of them." He looked up at Ahmed's face. "You were right. It was easy to build the bomb. We bought the parts at Walmart and Home Depot. We even tested the fuse."

"Who is this 'we' you talk about? Are you in gang?"

Kamal let a slight smile crease his lips and held up his hand. "No, no. Just a friend of mine who believes as I do."

Ahmed shook Kamal's shoulder. "And is he hurt like you? Did you kill him?"

Kamal pulled loose, stepped back, and held up his hand again. "No, nothing like that. He's fine. He helped me that's all. I guess it messed up his hearing for a day or two, but he's okay now. And I can't say about dreams. Why do you ask about them?"

Ahmed let a grin reveal his tobacco-stained teeth. "Kamal, I know many things. You do not understand. In Gaza I be like you. Much energy, hate, fire. I want to fight the infidels and make Allah proud. Now we in America. We safe. We can make a good life. No rockets here. No soldiers. Those things were for there. Not here." He frowned at Kamal. "My man, tell me you no want kill people here."

"Uncle, I cannot kill them all." Kamal wagged his finger. "But one person, he must die. Then I can rest."

"Who is this person you must kill?"

"Do you remember the store in the mall I told you about? In front of my leather goods place?" He watched for a sign of recognition from his uncle. Nothing. "Remember it's a Christian place where people come for prayer—to make them well, heal parts of their body? And it happens, all the time. They have crowds sometimes that wait for prayer. And it's free. Nobody pays, unless they donate money."

Ahmed frowned and put his finger to his lips, then raised his finger. "Ah, yes, I remember now. You want to blow up store. Make them stop."

"That's right. I still do. Even more than when I came to you last time."

"Who you want kill?"

"His name is Paul. He's the boss. The place is his project from his University."

"I never hear of this."

"Me either, but that's what he says. He's very friendly. He asks me about myself. I hate it. I hate him!" Kamal's face burned with rage. His fists clenched.

"Kamal, Kamal, is good to have anger. But you must be smart. America has good police. Many cameras take your picture that you don't even know. Do you want to die for Allah when you do this?"

Kamal sucked in his lower lip. "No, not really. I hadn't thought about that."

"Ah-ha. I understand. You want to be what they say, 'assassin.'"

Kamal hesitated. "I guess that's right." He looked at his uncle. He wanted to ask for his help, but was afraid to.

"And you want me help?"

"Could you?"

"And if I no help? You stop?"

"No, never!" Kamal raised a fist.

Ahmed sucked in a deep breath through his teeth. "Kamal, I no like this. You put me in hard place. I no help you with bomb. You almost kill yourself." He held his hand up, cutting off Kamal's possible protest. "So now you say you become assassin. Another thing you not know about. Okay, I must help you this time, so you still live."

"Thank you, Uncle. I will make you proud."

"How you want kill this man? Shoot him? Poison?"

"I think shoot him."

"Where? What are his habits?"

"I have no idea. Why? Does that make a difference?"

"Big difference. If you shoot him from far away, you need rifle. If you are close, pistol." Ahmed spoke as though instructing a child.

"Hm, I never realized that." He frowned. "I'd say 'close'. Can you help me get a gun?"

"Not yet. First, more questions. Where you be when you shoot him? In his place at mall? Where he live? In his car? Where you carry gun? Are police near where you shoot? In America some people have gun you no see. Will they see you with gun? Will this man be alone?"

"Not in the mall. Too many people." Kamal stopped to think again. "I am so glad you want to help me with this. I can understand that it's not simple. What do you suggest I do first?"

"Do you ever shoot pistol?"

"No, not really. Never."

"Okay, we start there. You must learn gun, how to shoot. How to be safe. How not to shoot bad thing—only what you want."

"So, I guess the first step is to buy a gun. How do you do that in America?"

"Buy gun not good idea. It tell FBI you have it. Wait here."

Kamal sat still as his uncle shuffled out of the room. All of his questions tumbled through his head. He had work to do, decisions to make. A minute or two later his uncle returned and held out a cardboard box.

"Here, you take."

The box was heavy. Kamal almost dropped it. He pulled back the flaps. A pistol and a box of ammunition. "Oh, praise Allah." He smiled at Ahmed. "You're giving this to me? Is it yours?"

"Yes, I give to you. I no need. It is good gun. Russian Gun. Be careful. It has bullets in it."

Kamal picked it up carefully and examined it. "It says 'Makarov, Bulgaria.'" He gripped the handle and slipped his finger through the trigger guard.

"Stop!" Ahmed barked and grabbed Kamal's gun hand. "Put down. Already you make mistake. I show you. I teach you safety now. Next you practice. Then you practice more. Then we talk again. Find out if you ready to kill."

Chapter 34

Paul held up his phone. "What happened Dad? Is there damage?"

"Whoa there, son. Security found the mall door broken. They flashed their lights in but didn't enter. I assume their protocol is to call the city police to go with them since they're not armed. Then they called me because I am the leasor of record."

"Makes sense. Thanks, Dad."

"Is there anything valuable there? Computers, money?"

"I'm not sure. Mary?" He looked at her. She had her ear next to his and heard his father too.

She shook her head. "No, I brought the donations box and computer home because it's Saturday night and we're closed Sunday. I count the money and archive the records from the computer." She pursed her lips. "Wait a minute. Jas has a laptop in the break area that we use for client reports. As I recall she keeps it in a drawer overnight."

"Thanks, Mary. I'll will relay it to Mall Security." Frank said, "Listen, kids, why don't you finish your evening, and then tomorrow afternoon we'll go to the mall and find out what happened. By then the police should be done with their search, and we can talk to security too. There's no need to go this evening. I don't know why, son, but I'm not worried. Whatever's happened, we'll take care of it. Not to worry."

Paul grinned and whispered to Mary, "'Not to worry' is my father's motto. He's often right." He spoke into the phone. "Okay Dad, I'll be home in a while," and hung up.

"Now, where were we?" Drawing her close, he wrapped his arms around her, and eased their faces together until they touched cheek to cheek. "Oh Mary, please forgive me. I realize I can be a bit intense. But tonight what's important is you. Thank you so much for your patience." And he gave her a long, lingering kiss. She returned it with passion.

***

Paul, his parents, and Mary gathered at The Prayer Place door Sunday afternoon. Police tape blocked the entrance. Paul peered through the door. Chairs were tipped over, Mary's desk drawers on the floor, and papers strewn about. Frank said, "Looks like kids' vandalism. Let's go up to the Mall office and hear what they have to tell us." He turned for the stairs, and the others followed as he expected.

Minutes later as they opened the office door, a youngish woman in tailored tan slacks and a cream-colored silk blouse opened it for them. "Mr. Shepard, good to see you again. I wish it were under happier circumstances." She turned to Marina, "You must be Mrs. Shepard. I'm Gloria Sherwood, the mall manager. I normally don't work Sunday, but this kind of break-in is a rare occurrence."

Paul's mother accepted Gloria's handshake. "Gloria, I'm Marina. Hopefully the next time we meet it will be a happier situation."

"Yes, me too. But we're lucky today. We have a few seconds of security camera footage that may be helpful. We'd like you to look at it."

"Good!" Paul exclaimed. "Let's see what you got."

Gloria introduced a security officer who'd just arrived. "This is Gordon Wishman, our Director of Security." His buzz haircut complimented his blue uniform shirt. Although middle aged judging from his overdeveloped pecs and biceps he'd obviously kept in good condition. "

They all shook hands. Gordon explained. "There are two cameras that cover your section of the mall. They blacked out the first one with spray paint. However, they either didn't notice the other one, or decided it was too far away to matter."

He led them to a computer monitor in a side office. "If you can slide around so you can all view it, I'll play what we have. The light's low because it's outside our business hours. This happened at ten PM last night. By the way, the reason we have this clip is that the camera is motion activated. It roams its visible space until it senses motion."

"Impressive." Frank said.

The camera looked down the mall in front of The Prayer Place, Kamal's leather goods kiosk visible on the left. Two figures appeared out of the dim background and scurried to the recessed door of The Prayer Place.

"That's Blade!" Mary yelped.

Gordon stopped the tape. "You recognize him?"

"Yes. He and his buddies came into the store to hassle me one Friday evening a couple of weeks ago. Then a few nights later they did the same thing out in the parking lot. I don't know the other guy's name, but I recognize him too."

"You called him Blade."

"That's what his buddies called him. I'm sure that's not his name, but I have no idea what it really is."

"Deshawn Silver," Gordon said. "He's well known to us." He turned to her. "Are you sure it's him?"

She nodded. "Very sure, he got right in my face in the store, and pulled a knife on me in the parking lot."

"May I ask why he'd didn't follow through in the parking lot?"

Mary and Paul exchanged glances. "Paul came up— with a gun."

Paul leaped into the conversation. "I carry. I have a permit."

"Fine," Gordon replied. "I'll need to get all this down and see your permit before you leave."

"No problem." Paul answered.

"What happened in the store?" Frank asked, "We looked through the window, but couldn't see much."

Gloria said, "We'd like you to examine the store and identify anything taken. Mostly they threw things around and made a mess. I think they broke one chair, but that's all we found."

Gordon added, "They were there twelve minutes. We have them on tape as they left. They faced away from the camera on their way out so there's nothing to see."

"How did they get in after hours?" Marina asked.

"Good question, Mother," Frank patted her on the arm.

"We think they hid someplace after the mall closed, a men's room stall with their feet up or possibly a service closet. Then they came out to do their deed and left through one of the fire doors. This was not a spontaneous incident. They planned it."

"Mr. Blade didn't like being run off—twice." Paul said.

***

As they walked through The Prayer Place Mary went straight to the break area and pulled open a drawer. "Hah! They missed it!" She held up a laptop. "Jas's computer. Praise God." She surveyed the area. "Where's the Keurig?" It was gone.

Gordon smiled. "Hm, I guess they felt they had to take something, even a coffee maker. Skimpy haul I'd say. Blade won't feel vindicated."

"What'll happen to him?" Frank asked.

"Oh." Gordon smiled. "He's over eighteen and will be tried as an adult. We've waited for an opportunity like this for some time. Thanks to this young lady here, he'll go to jail, maybe prison."

Frank put his arm around Paul's shoulder as they walked out. "See son, not to worry."

Chapter 35

Paul, Mary, Loretta, and Jas filed into Pastor Sandy Oates' office. Paul's fists clenched. "Pastor, we've got a real situation here and need your help."

Pastor Oates rose from his desk and came around to greet them. "Paul, good to see you again, you too Loretta and Mary. And you, young lady. I saw you at the picnic, but we haven't been introduced. I'm..." He stopped himself. "Well, I guess you know who I am. And you are?"

"Jas, full name Jaslyn Malka. It's Coptic."

"That's interesting. I'm sure there's a story there, but we'll save it for another time." He waved toward his conference table. "Grab a seat. But before we get into your issue, let me say we're all very proud and excited about your work at The Prayer Place. To be honest, Paul, when your dad first suggested it as a ministry the church might want to get involved in, I thought, 'Sure, why not? Might as well give it a shot.'" He laughed. "I had no idea what a success it'd become—or what a variety of opposition you'd face. Your parents keep me up to date. So, that being said, who can tell me what brings you here today?"

Paul sat up. "Several weeks ago, two unusual ladies came by, an albino and a Goth. Turned out they were witches. They didn't want prayer. They seemed curious and I suspect were checking us out. Loretta, can you tell Sandy what you learned during that visit?"

Loretta smiled at Sandy. "Well, you know me. I'm always chatting about something."

Sandy smiled and nodded.

"While this lady, Sybil, sat next to me in the waiting room I don't why, but I talked about all the problems I had with my fifth pregnancy, God's miraculous healings and how I became a believer. I told her all that. It felt like the right thing to do. She seemed so lost. Anyway, as they were about to leave, I asked her if she was pregnant, and she was. I was pretty sure of that before I asked. And she was having a hard first trimester. So I prayed for her right there in the waiting room. That was all."

Sandy smiled. "My my, Loretta, I wasn't aware that you were so bold."

She blushed.

Paul eyed Mary. "Then about two weeks later?"

Mary nodded. "They both came back, and after the albino, Vestal left, Sybil asked to speak to Loretta." He looked at the three women, "Who wants to take it from here?"

Jas leaned forward. "When she came to Loretta and me to pray for her pregnancy, she mentioned that it wasn't her first one. When we asked what happened, she said 'He didn't make it.' We weren't clear what she meant, so we passed on it for the moment. When Loretta asked if she was familiar with God, and she said not really, so Loretta spoke scriptures from The Father's Love for her. Sybil was almost in tears."

Loretta nodded. "I love to do that. Anyway, later I asked her what happened to her first baby, she said he'd been sacrificed. I was shocked. Jas too."

Jas pursed her lips. "Neither one of us knew where to go with that, and since we'd
been with her for almost forty minutes, we ended the session soon afterward."

She added, "After Sybil left, Loretta and I talked about what she meant by sacrificed, and concluded she meant that she, or someone, had killed him. Could it have been in some kind of ceremony? Neither of us are familiar with witchcraft, so we didn't know what else it could be. Anyway, I told Paul, and he said we'd have to tell you. So here we are."

Sandy raised his eyebrows. "Wow. That's quite a story. I'd say 'amazing'. It seems like it must be true. I mean, is there any reason to suspect she's deranged or confused?" Both ladies shook their heads.

"Okay, which of you is the main person she has confidence in, talks to the most?"

Jas said, "Oh Loretta, for sure."

"Okay," he continued, "Loretta, the most important thing here is that this lady comes to Jesus as her Lord and Savior." Loretta nodded. "I take it you did not get that far on the last visit?"

"No, Pastor. I would say not. She was receptive and received the Word of God in The Father's Love well, but not to the point of commitment. And, to be honest, I didn't push it. Was that a mistake?"

Sandy shook his head. "Not at all. You have good instincts and listen to the Lord's prompting. You made a good start." He paused then added, "What I'm thinking here is you should call her and see if you can continue the conversation. Try to get her to come back to The Prayer Place."

Mary interrupted. "That's a problem. Neither of them wanted to fill out our information forms. Sybil finally did, but I wouldn't be surprised if she fabricated her information, maybe even her name. For instance she didn't include a phone number, and gave an Indiana address, a rural route. Not here in Ohio.

"Nuts," Sandy said. "So you're dependent on their coming back?" They all nodded. "Okay, then we pray for Sybil's salvation and that she returns."

"And if she does come back?" Paul asked.

"Most important is that she comes to the Lord. That comes first. Assuming you're successful there, then I suggest Loretta probe what she meant when she said she'd sacrificed her first baby. If she confirms that your suspicions are correct, that she or someone killed the baby, then in the eyes of the law, it's murder. You with me this far?" Jas and Loretta nodded. Loretta wiped her eyes. "If that's the case, this is very serious. She could do it again. She needs to tell the police what happened."

Loretta sighed. "Lord, help me."

"He will, Loretta. He will." Sandy patted her hand.

"What if Sybil refuses, won't do it?" Paul asked.

"Then Loretta says she'll call them."

Chapter 36

Anton opened the door to The Prayer Place, to let two of his friends in. They approached Mary at the sign-in station. It was now a counter instead of a temporary table. "Hi Mary, remember me, Anton Bjornson?"

Mary's face erupted in a broad grin. "I sure do! Anton, does this mean what I think it does?" She held out her hand.

Anton took it in both of his. "It sure does. Normal counts. No more HIV." His eyes glistened. "I still can't believe it, but the test doesn't lie—especially four times in a row, two weeks apart."

"Praise God!" Mary exclaimed. "That is such wonderful news. You know you're the first person to come in with HIV. This is marvelous." She looked at his two friends. "How about that, gentlemen? Is God good or what?"

They both smiled and nodded. The first was medium height, thin brown hair, blue eyes, delicate features, a tan polo shirt and pressed chinos. "I'm Terry Branigan. And yes, I'd like prayer for HIV too."

Mary smiled. "Pleased to meet you, Terry." She handed him a clipboard with their information form on it. "If you'd have a seat over there and fill this out." She looked at the third member of the group. "Are you here for prayer too, or just moral support for Terry?"

A slight blush swept over the man's face. "Oh, I need prayer, but not for HIV. I guess I need to fill out a form too." He reached for a clip-board. "My name is Xenos Cristophos." He looked at Anton. "And no, Anton, I am not Irish." His gaze returned to Mary. "Anton likes to claim I'm Irish when I introduce myself." He was short, burly, with black, curly hair and a well-trimmed moustache. He wore a short-sleeved knit shirt that showed off his hairy, muscular forearms.

Mary said, "I'll tell Paul you're healed, Anton. He'll be excited. It helps us to keep up our faith up when we learn people are healed after they leave."

Anton said, "I kind of hoped to tell him myself."

"Oh, how silly of me. Of course." She looked at her computer. "He's with a client at the moment, so I'll leave him a note that he has a visitor. How's that?"

Anton grinned again. "That's great."

***

Paul came around the corner and stopped in his tracks. "Anton! You're back. Hallelujah." He strode over. Anton stood, and they gripped hands like old friends.

Anton said, "Yep, normal counts, three weeks now. My doctor doesn't understand it, but I'm off all meds and feel great." He turned to his guests. "I brought a couple of friends who are aware of what happened to me and they want prayer too." He introduced Terry and Xenos.

Paul reached for their completed forms. "Terry, I see you want God to repeat what He did for Anton."

"Yes, please."

"Well, all we do is command the condition to leave. The power comes from the Holy Spirit. I see you have a Pentecostal background."

"That's how I grew up. They weren't too happy with my, ah, lifestyle since I came out, but that's history now."

"No problem here." Paul replied. He led them to Mary's desk. "Mary, could I meet with Terry here?"

She grinned. "Yes sir, mister director. In fact, I recommend it." She reached out and squeezed his hand. "Want to pair up with Julius again?"

"Sure." He looked at Terry, then Anton. "Anton, do you want to observe, or what?"

"That'd be great."

Paul asked Mary, "Who do we have for Xenos?"

She looked at his form. "Xenos? I like that name. May I ask if a female staff member would be okay as part of the team? I mean, is this a guy thing?"

Xenos frowned and scratched his chin. "I guess it'd be okay. It's not what you call 'a guy thing.'"

She looked at Paul. "How about Gil and Jas?"

"Good team," he confirmed.

***

A few minutes later Gil Martenelli and Jas stepped around the corner into the waiting area. Gil was an experienced volunteer from the church, with gray-flecked brown hair, a goatee, tanned, narrow cheeks and dark brown eyes. He held up a form. "Xenos?"

Xenos stood. "That's me. Do I follow you?"

"If you would, sir," Gil said, as he offered his hand. "I'm Gil. Pleased to meet you. And welcome to The Prayer Place. We've seen incredible things all summer long."

"That's great. And why I'm here. You prayed and Anton's HIV free."

Gil glanced at the form. "But that's not why you're here, right?"

"No, it's a little complicated."

As they entered their assigned prayer room, Jas held out her hand. "Hi! I'm Jas, the other half of your prayer team." She reached for the form from Gil. "Your form is rather cryptic. So, what's going on?"

Xenos stared at the floor, then each of them. "To be honest, I must be going crazy. Several months ago, these violent dreams showed up. I mean gross. They always woke me up. But now it comes over me while I'm awake. It takes me by surprise, and I have no clue what to do."

Gil held his hands up. "What kind of violence? How does it show up?"

Xenos eyebrows arched and he took a deep breath. "I get incredibly agitated, consumed with hostility and hatred. In my dreams I find a knife in my hands and I slash people. I mean cut them all over—like their face, their arms, their body. That's when I wake up."

"Wow," Jas said, and she looked at Gil like she wanted him to take the lead.

"And when you're awake, is it the same thing?"

"Almost. I used to carry a pocket knife but have stopped." His eyes filled, and he looked ready to cry. "I don't want to kill anyone, or hurt them. I don't trust myself anymore."

"So, then what happens?" Gil asked.

Xenos pursed his lips. "I have a Greek restaurant over on Madison Avenue. Well, for instance yesterday, I met with some of my staff. We all sat in the break area, and the hostility started again. Like I wanted to leap over the table and tear someone's eyes out. I had to excuse myself and leave. I hid in my office until I got myself together." His eyes beseeched Gil and Jas. "You gotta' help me here."

Gil reached out. "Can I put my hand on your shoulder?"

Xenos nodded.

"Xenos, Jesus can help you. He's not the author of these horrible feelings. You said this started several months ago. Did anything unusual happen around that time?"

"Well, yeah, my dad died. He was eighty-eight. He started the restaurant and ran it for years. Eventually I took over. It's been quite successful." He looked at Gil. "Is it possible that had anything to do with it?

Gil nodded. "It could be. Did anything else happen in that period?"

Xenos's brow furrowed. "No, not that I recall."

"Is your mother still alive?"

"Oh no, she died while I was still a kid. We came from Greece a few years before that. To tell the truth, I believe my father worked her to death to get the restaurant established."

"And how did that affect you?"

"I missed my mom of course—a lot. And, I guess I was mad at my dad."

"Did you ever talk to him about it?"

"No way. Nobody ever said a thing to my dad. He had a temper like a volcano. You could never predict when it would go off."

"So how did you handle it?"

"I just tried to stay out of his way. And his reach. And do what he said." Xenos stopped talking. "After a while I got as big as he was. So he decided to teach me to take over the restaurant. We became more like—buddies, or maybe business partners."

"Did you ever talk about your mother?"

"No, never. I never talked about her to anyone."

"Do you have any brothers or sisters?"

"My older sister, Ellie, but she left as soon as she turned eighteen. We almost never hear from her."

Gil glanced over at Jas, who remained expressionless, then turned to their guest. "Xenos, let me tell you what I suspect is happening here, and you tell me if it seems right."

"Okay."

"It looks to me like a spirit entered you around the time of your mother's death. As you tell it, you had no outlets for your grief, and a cold, unsupportive father. He undoubtedly struggled with his own grief, but he's not here today. Remember, you were very vulnerable then. You must have had a lot of anger and bitterness, mostly toward your dad. But you couldn't let them out—until he died. Then this murderous spirit revealed itself." He stopped to examine Xenos. "Did you ever consider killing your father?"

Tears flowed down Xenos's cheeks. "Yes, especially as a kid. Daddy was so mean." He looked at Gil. "But I couldn't. I mean, kill my dad? Where would I go? What could I do?"

"So you were stuck. Big time." Gil handed him a box of tissues.

"Big time." Xenos nodded, blew his nose and wiped his eyes.

Gil laid his hand on Xenos's shoulder. "Are you okay? Do you want to keep going here, or do you need a break? Are we on the right track?"

"Absolutely, let's do this. What happens now?"

"Now we'll lead you in a prayer of deliverance and forgiveness, and get this 'spirit thing' gone forever. This will take some time." He turned to Jas. "Can you tell Mary we're doing a deliverance, and we need a double appointment?" She nodded and left the room. Moments later she returned with three bottles of water. Gil smiled, "Thanks Jas. Great idea." He cracked one open and took a good swig. Xenos did too.

***

As they left the prayer room Xenos beamed and looked ready to skip. "Unbelievable. How did you do that? I'm positive that thing is gone. I don't need to be afraid to go to sleep anymore."

"We don't get the credit my friend, Jesus does. He's the one who gave all of us authority over demons and all the power of the enemy. He really loves you." Gil paused and pointed to Xenos. "You need to come back to him."

Xenos stared at Gil. "Gil, you're right. I know what He says about my lifestyle. That needs to change."

"It sure does, my friend. It sure does." Gil smiled.

Xenos gripped Gil's arm. "By the way, I'm not supposed to tell you this, but do you remember Hank Polaski who was here with Anton?"

"I'm not sure. But what about him?"

"He plans to lead an LGBT demonstration here to accuse you of homophobia. I think this Saturday afternoon. They plan to get a TV station to cover it."

Chapter 37

Dr. Hudson eased open the door to Tony's office, spotted him, and stepped in. He took a step back. Who was the good-looking woman parked in front of his desk? Tony Ziparelli rose to his feet. "Charlie, how are you? Thanks for coming by." He turned to the lady. "This is Emma Ratliff, AKA many things. She's my, ah, associate. Emma, this is Dr. Charles Hudson." Middle-aged, medium height, light brown straight hair, modest makeup, and a form-fitting red dress,

She smiled, stood and shook his hand. "My pleasure, doctor." She sat back down and tugged her dress over her knees.

Charlie pulled up a chair. As usual, Tony's office smelled of cigars, despite the empty ashtrays. He frowned at Tony. "Why do I sense we're not having a victory party?"

Tony smiled. "Because, my friend, you're a perceptive man." He shot a glance at Emma, then back to the doctor. "Okay, when you and I talked I told you to do nothing, I'd take it from here."

"Right." Charlie intoned. "And I didn't do anything—other than lose another surgery due to that blasted Prayer Place."

"Oh no. So sorry."

"Yeah, me too, of course. This one was incredible. Several years ago, I patched up a kid's leg with some screws, a little wire, and a short plate. Recently he said they ached and since his bones had knit together well, he wanted me to take them out. Great, no problem. I do it often. Then he calls me. 'Doc, can you x-ray my leg again? I went to The Prayer Place, and I think I'm fine now. It doesn't hurt.' So I did

Tony, it was blanko—no screws, no wire, no plate. I checked his leg to be sure someone else hadn't done it. Smooth as a newborn baby's bottom. No new scars, no swelling, no pain." He stared at Tony. "I feel like I'm competing with God."

Tony's brow wrinkled. "Hm, I can see that. It sure does." He took a deep breath. "Anyway, I told Emma here what our situation was, and that we wanted to record them giving medical advice. Let me say I have a lot of confidence in this lady. She's very talented. She understood what we wanted right away and agreed to help us. Emma, do you want to take it from here?"

She colored slightly at his compliment and nodded. "Sure. Okay, Doc, I figured this would be a snap. I scoped out the joint a couple of days ahead. A bunch of college kids, and senior-type people work there as far as I could tell. So I posed as a frazzled dingbat. With a wire of course, which I tested in advance—no interference. I've done this kind of, ah, let me say I assumed this would be easy."

She checked out Tony and Charlie. "You with me so far?" They nodded. "Okay, so when I got in there, I gave it my best shot. The receptionist put me with a young gal and an older lady. They were both very nice and polite. They listened to my tale of woe."

Tony interrupted, "As far as I'm concerned, she gave it the good old college try."

Charlie grimaced. "Great."

"Thanks, Tony. I appreciate it. Anyway, they wouldn't bite. They were well trained, I guess. Told me they didn't give medical advice, only prayer." She held out her hands in surrender. "I kept it up. I switched subjects and did my best needy, hopeless, confused lady." She stopped, looked at both men, clenched her fists. "Then this young gal called me on it.'

Charlie said, "Excuse me? What's that mean?"

Tony interrupted. "We've got the tape here. Is this a good time to play it? That'll clear it up." Charlie nodded, as Tony put a small tape player on his desk, popped in a diskette and punched a button.

When the tape finished, Charlie's eyebrows arched, "Wow. Emma, you sure sounded real to me. What happened?"

"When this chick said, 'Who do you work for? Who sent you to do this?' I knew I was toast. I heard that last line on the way out the door."

She held her chin with her thumb and forefinger and tugged on an ear. "It's almost like they knew ahead of time. Like they'd been warned or something."

"How is that possible?" Charlie asked. His eyes connected with Tony's.

Tony shrugged and held out his palms. "Well, I know what my wife'd say."

"What?"

"God told them." He looked at his client. "Doc, you gotta admit there's some spooky stuff at that place. Looks to me like it's for real."

Charlie nodded. "In which case I get the short end of the stick." A broad grin spread across his face. "You know what I need to do now?"

"No clue."

"Find an atheist insurance company and get a policy that covers me for damages from acts of God."

Chapter 38

Kamal approached the door to the target range with his uncle Ahmed. Popping sounds penetrated the double paned glass as several people fired in their booths, including three women. That was a surprise. Were there more? Although Kamal had preliminary instruction in Ahmed's apartment, he still felt nervous. He hoped his hand wouldn't shake.

Ahmed taught Kamal how to carry the Makarov, load and unload it, how to sight a target, and set the safety. He also taught him the hazards of target selection and how to shoot. Kamal was excited about shooting for the first time. He'd bought enough ammunition at the gun store to get access to the range.

The range issued them standard eye and ear protection. He carried his weapon in the same container his uncle had stored it in. They entered the range and put on their ear protection. The other shooters had fabric range bags or plastic gun cases on the counters behind them. He had a cardboard box. No matter. He only planned to shoot one time for real.

The range master put them in booth number seven, so Kamal unloaded his box on the counter behind it. Ahmed flattened out their human outline targets. The range master showed them how to work the overhead target carrier. Ahmed seemed familiar with it, clipped on the first target, and ran it out to twenty-five feet.

Kamal stepped up to the shooter's bench with his gun. He held the ammunition magazine in his other hand. The floor around and in front of him was covered with empty shell casings. As he was about to shove the loaded magazine into the butt of the gun, his uncle gripped his hand. "No, not yet. First, I want you aim and pull trigger at target with no shoot."

Kamal squared off in front of the bench, bent both knees, and held the gun in both hands. Then he jerked the trigger and the gun's hammer clicked.

Ahmed stepped up behind him and said in his ear, "Squeeze, not jerk. And hold other hand lower, so slide does not cut it. Now, do again."

Kamal took a breath, held the gun as steadily as possible, and squeezed the trigger.

"Good. Now put in bullets."

He inserted the magazine in the butt of the gun and slapped it with his spare hand. "Now, shoot one time— at target. Aim for heart."

The target seemed far away. Kamal held the gun as motionless as he was able and pulled the trigger. It would not move. He turned to see his uncle smile, then tap his head with his forefinger. Oh yes, he forgot to rack the slide and put the first shell in the firing chamber. He racked the shell into position, took careful aim, and pulled the trigger. The gun banged, spit fire and jerked his hand back. Ahmed told him it was supposed to, but it still surprised him. Hm, was there was a hole above the target man's left shoulder?

Ahmed yelled in his ear. "Now you practice. Shoot five more times and we look at target."

Kamal gripped the gun hard and squeezed off five more rounds. He knew the spent cartridge casings flew out of the side of the weapon with each shot, but paid them no attention. When he retrieved the target, it had four bullet holes, scattered around. One hit in the black circle of the chest area.

"Finish magazine."

As he fired the last round the slide locked open, exposing the firing chamber. He didn't expect that and examined it. He pushed the release for the empty magazine which dropped on the floor. He could see right through the gun. Curious, he picked up a fresh casing. It was so hot he dropped it instantly. He touched the barrel, and it was very warm too.

Ahmed said. "Give me next magazine and I try. Need to test sights." He ran the target back out to twenty-five feet, slapped the last loaded magazine into the gun, racked the slide, and fired off six spaced shots. When he retrieved the target, the center ring on the man's chest was full of holes. Ahmed handed him the weapon. "Gun still good. You practice now. I reload magazine for you."

Their hour of range time ended as they'd exhausted Kamal's ammunition and perforated both targets. On the drive back to Ahmed's apartment Ahmed asked. "This person you want to kill, he wear body armor?"

Kamal shook his head in surprise. "No, I'm sure he doesn't."

"Good. He have armed guards with him?"

"Also no. For sure. Why do you ask?"

"Because, Kamal, you need much practice to be good shooter with my gun. I think you need make very good plan to have success."

"Okay, what should be the main part of the plan?"

"Two things. Aim for heart, not head. And get close, very close to shoot."

Chapter 39

Loretta spotted Sybil through the front wall glass. "Praise God. She's back." she said to nobody in particular.

She stepped to the door to greet her. "Sybil! I hardly recognized you. All the Goth makeup, the studs, the earrings—gone. I love your new look. For me, it's far better. Do you like it?" She squeezed Sybil's hand.

Sybil blushed and looked at the floor. "Well, I'm still kinda' getting used to it." She looked at Loretta again. "It sure is easier to get up in the morning." A faint smile crossed her lips.

Loretta turned to face Mary and mouthed 'Get Paul'. Mary nodded and disappeared toward the back.

She grinned back at Sybil. "I'm so happy to see you again. This is an answer to prayer."

"No way." Sybil frowned and tucked in her chin.

"Oh yes, I prayed you'd come back. I wanted to call you–to see how you were doing. But there was no phone number on your form."

"Yeah. Well, sorry about that. In fact, none of that form is the truth. Vestal didn't want to let on who we are, or where we live."

"I remember you said you lived in Indiana. Was that right?"

"Yeah. Only that part."

"So, Sybil, are you here for prayer, this time?"

She scratched her foot on the floor. "Yes, I guess I am. After my last visit I was all stirred up. You and Jas gave me a lot to think about, and you touched me. It's ... it's like my mind's been in a fog."

"A fog?"

"Yeah. I've been on pot for quite a while, actually most of my life. And listening to Satanic music a lot. Drinking too, quite a bit. After we met, I got to thinking if I'm gonna to keep this baby I'd best clean up my act for its sake. So, no more pot, no more booze. And guess what? I feel a lot better too."

"I'm sure you do. That's marvelous." Paul stood nearby. "Sybil, have you ever met Paul Shepard? He's our director and the founder of The Prayer Place."

"No." She shot a quick glance up at him. Her voice was barely audible. "Hi Paul."

Paul extended his hand, "Hi Sybil. It's a pleasure to meet you. Loretta suggested that I join you if you returned."

Sybil stepped back and frowned. "She did?"

Loretta nodded. "Yep. Paul loves to share the love of Jesus, and I figured you'd like that." She paused. "Tell you what, Sybil, could you fill out the form again with the right information?" Sybil nodded. "Great, I'll sit with you and then we'll go to a prayer room together, okay?"

"Yeah." She nodded, picked up a clipboard, sat down, and started to write.

As they settled in a prayer room Paul and Loretta examined her form. He said, "I guess this is out in the country."

"Yep, I live in an old farm house. Most of the farm part has fallen down, but the house still works, more or less. I have electricity, and that's about it."

"And what county is it?"

"Ah, Mitchell County."

"And how did you come to live there?"

"Oh, it was my mom's house. She died when I was fourteen—crystal meth. But I stayed on. Didn't have no place else to go. "

Paul asked, "Was there someone, ah, someone to look after you?"

"Well sort of. My cousin, Vonnie, she's older than me. She'd come over regular, bring food, help me with stuff. It was kinda rough." Sybil looked at the ceiling and squinted. "She's the one what started me in the Coven."

"The coven?" Paul and Loretta chorused.

"Yeah, well, witchcraft. They met regular all year long. They'd come get me, let me be part of their meetings. Sometimes they'd have parties. I'd go too. It was sorta of like, family."

Paul said, "I guess it was all women?"

"Almost. Vonnie had some brothers who hung out with her. One of them, Zack, he wasn't her real brother. That's just what she said. Anyway, he took a shine to me, and, well, that's where the first baby come from."

Paul said, "I'd like to hear about that, but first, can I ask how you and God are doing?"

She shrugged. "Okay, I guess. I don't know much about God or any of that stuff. I can't hardly remember church as a girl."

"But you went to church?"

"Sometimes. Big white one. Baptist maybe? Yeah. Most times I'd go to Sunday school with some other kids, but sometimes I'd sit with my mom. It was okay. They had good snacks."

"Do you remember what they talked about?"

"Hm, let me see. There was some guy got swallowed up by a big fish and then dumped on the shore. I forget his name."

Loretta said, "Jonah. God sent him to preach to the people in Nineveh."

"Yeah, that was quite a story. Oh yeah. I remember when Jesus walked on the water to get in a boat. Didn't some other guy try it too, but started to sink?"

Loretta rested her hand on Sybil's shoulder. "You remember a lot. I'm impressed. Do you remember who Jesus is?"

"Gee, wasn't he s'posed to be, ah, God's Son or something?" She looked to Loretta for confirmation.

"That's right. Would you like me to tell you why God sent His only Son to us?"

Sybil sighed and nodded. "I guess. Okay."

Loretta related the gospel story for her with slow and precise, simple language. "So you see, He sent His most precious possession, His son, to save us from our sins and give us a promise of life with Him forever."

Sybil nodded and pursed her lips.

"What's going on?"

"This is all so new to me. It's like from another world." She smiled at Loretta.

"Would you like his promises for yourself?"

"Yeah. Yeah, I do." Sybil's smiled broadened.

Loretta looked at Paul, who indicated that she should continue. "That's great. How about I'll say a simple prayer, line by line? You repeat it after me. And stop me if there's anything you're not sure about. Okay?"

Sybil nodded.

"Sybil, this will be the most important thing you do in your life. Are you ready?"

Sybil looked at her with tears in her eyes. "Yes I am."

Loretta began. *Dear Jesus, I confess I done a lot of bad things in my life. And I've kept you out of my life.* She stopped when Sybil's tears made it impossible for her to continue.

"I'm real, real sorry and I want to fix it. I want to repent and ask You to forgive me. Come into my heart, Lord Jesus, and be my Savior forever. Amen—she broke down and sobbed.

Loretta hugged and held her for a long time. Eventually Sybil released her, leaned back, and grinned. She looked at Paul.

He grinned back. "I am so proud of you, Sybil, so very proud. That was wonderful."

"Thanks Paul."

He reached for her hand. "Sybil, if you can stay a while longer, we have a couple more things we'd like to cover."

"Oh-kay," she said with a slight wince.

"Good. As you describe your living situation, you live alone, and right now hang out with people who aren't good for you anymore. Does that sound about right?"

"Yeah, I never thought of it like that."

"Well, I'd like to get you plugged in to a good church with people who can come and help you, answer your questions, and support you in healthy, Christian ways."

"Hey, that sounds good, but I have no idea ..."

Paul patted her shoulder. "Not to worry, Sybil. We'll help you. I'll talk to my pastor who knows a lot of people. And we'll try to come up with something right away. Does that sound reasonable?"

She took a deep breath and smiled at him. "Nobody's ever done that before. That'd be great."

He held out her form. "This phone number. Your cell right?" She nodded. "And it works where you live? We can call you there?" She nodded again.

"Good. Okay. The other thing is what you mentioned here earlier, your first baby. Could you tell us what happened to that baby?"

"Oh boy." She paused, took a deep breath. "I guess I need to. Okay, first of all, I was stoned most of the time in those days. That's how I got pregnant. Hardly knew what I was doing."

"And where was the baby born?"

"In my bathtub. Wasn't nobody there but me and the baby. I was screaming and crying, and after she came out, so was she."

"So, it was a girl. Was she okay?"

"I think so. I didn't know nothing about having babies, but there she was. Then all that other stuff came out of me after she was born. We was a mess. So I cut her cord with a scissors, held it shut with a hairpin, and cleaned us both up. I didn't have no baby food, so I let her suck on me. I was pretty big by then, and there was plenty of milk. I got us into my bed, smoked a joint, and we both fell asleep. The next day I called Vonnie and told her about it." Sybil frowned. "Lemme see. Yeah, she come over and asked me what I wanted to do with the baby? Did I want to keep it?" Paul and Loretta looked at each other.

"I said 'not really', 'cause what was I going to do with her? Vonnie told me she could take the baby, and they'd sacrifice her to Molech, whoever that is, at the next coven meeting. It was only a couple days away. Would that be okay?"

Sybil looked at Loretta, who was wiping her eyes, then Paul. "Well, Vonnie was the one friend in the world I had and I sure didn't want to lose her, so I said okay, take the baby."

Loretta spoke in a soft, gentle voice. "And did you go to the meeting, dear?"

"Yeah, Vonnie picked me up. She had the baby asleep in the back seat in a box. Vonnie said she put something in her bottle to help her sleep. So, when we got there they had a big pile of wood out in the yard. Vonnie put the box right on top of the pile. We were almost the last ones to get there, so they started right away. As usual, I was pretty stoned, so I don't remember too good. They played some music, and we sang a chant kind of thing. One girl come out in a fancy costume, like a goddess or something, and said a bunch of stuff. She sprinkled something around the ground and on us. I guess it was blood. Anyway, then the wood started to burn somehow from down inside the pile. Before long it was roaring. The baby woke up and screamed, and then it stopped. The flames went way up in the air, and the box disappeared. After a long time the fire died down to ashes. I seen no bones or nothing. Then there was more chants and stuff, and we went home."

Paul shook his head. "Jesus, help us. Sybil, I've never heard of anything like this in my life. It's horrible."

Sybil hugged herself, doubled over, and wailed. "I know, I know. I didn't want to think about it then. I was stupid, stupid, stupid."

Paul knelt in front of her chair and took both her hands in his. He gazed into her eyes. "Sybil, now that you've taken Jesus as your Lord and Savior, He will forgive you of your sins. But you must still bear the consequences of them." He paused and studied her. "Do you understand that?"

Between her sobs she nodded. "Yes."

"Sybil, what you described is a crime. It must be reported."

She reared back, looked at him, eyes wide. "What, what do you mean?"

Paul took a deep breath and spoke in a very gentle voice. "This story, that you told us must be reported to law enforcement. Can you do that?"

"What?" She raised up, wild eyed. "No, no, I can't do that! No way. I can't."

Paul squeezed her hands. "Sybil, remember God loves you the way you are right now, here in this room. And Jesus forgives you for the sins you confessed. That's the most important thing. Sybil, if Loretta and I come with you, do you think you could tell it again?"

She nodded. "I guess I can try." She looked at them. "You promise you'll be there?"

"Yes. Absolutely." They both hugged her. "You are a strong woman, Sybil, very strong. We're going to be sure you're okay."

Tears streamed down her cheeks. 'Wow. I can't believe all this. It's amazing, absolutely amazing. Thank you so much."

"Thank you, Sybil, and thank you, Jesus."

***

After she left, Loretta bit her lip and tugged at her hair as she turned to Paul, her eyebrows drawn together. "What'll we do if she changes her mind?"

Chapter 40

Gordon Remington, Director of Mall Security, plopped down in the chair opposite Gloria Sherwood's desk. "Hi boss, have you heard the latest from The Prayer Place?"

Her eyes jerked up, wide open. "No. Now what?"

Gordon smiled. "Nothing we can't handle. One of Paul's guests gave him a heads-up that an LGBT group is planning a demonstration here Saturday afternoon, complete with TV coverage."

"Oh my. That's not what we need, not what we need at all. Nobody's notified us. Are you ready for it?"

"Just getting started." He held out his hand to reassure her, and smiled, "Here's what I want to do. First, I'll ask Paul to see if he can get more details. I'll also check in with a source who may have more info and then we'll coordinate with the city police to be sure we're ready to, shall we say, give them an appropriate welcome. They won't make it through a single door. Trust me."

Gloria smiled. "Gordon, I don't know what I'd do without you. Do I want all the details?"

"No, not really." He smirked. "Be here Saturday afternoon if you want a ringside seat. I assume you want to keep that Prayer Place in business."

"Are you kidding? They're the best thing that's happened to this mall all year. They bring in people from three states, folks that would never come here otherwise. And when they come for prayer, what else do they do? They eat, and they shop. And if they're healed, they may need new clothes or shoes or whatnot. Yes, Gordon, max protection for them."

"You got it, boss."

Minutes later Gordon stopped in speak to Paul. "Paul, Gordon Remington. Got a minute?"

Paul glanced at Mary, who frowned. "Yes, that's all I have. What's up?"

"You mentioned a possible LGBT demonstration this Saturday. Is there any way you can provide more details? Such as what time, what entrance they will try? Then I'll put together a plan to keep them outside the mall."

"I dunno' Gordon. Let me see what I can do." Mary searched her computer. "Xenos' number?" She nodded, copied a number on a post-it and gave it to him.

"Is she good or what?" Paul said to Gordon. "She's the glue that holds this project together." He paused, glanced at her. "And cute too."

Gordon smiled. "I can see that. Great. Okay, I'll let you go. Keep me posted on what you find. You got my number?"

"I'll put it in my speed dial right now. It's always something, isn't it?"

He nodded. "Sure is. By the way, Gloria mentioned that you folks are the best thing that has happened to this mall all year."

Paul grinned. "Really? Gee, thanks. God gets the glory, not us."

"You're gonna make a believer of me, aren't you?"

Paul beamed and gripped Gordon's substantial bicep. "I'd love to."

***

Saturday afternoon Paul stood next to Gordon near the mall's main entrance. Gloria observed from a few steps behind them. Paul glanced at his watch. "Almost two o'clock. Any sign of them?"

Gordon pointed. "Check out the two guys over by the big flower pots. See what they're holding?"

"Looks like a big umbrella. Makes little sense on a sunny day like today."

"It does if it's a banner. Anything else?"

"He's on his cell phone, scanning around the parking lot."

"Any guess what for?"

"No clue, Gordon. What do you think?"

"They're scouts. I'd guess they're waiting for media to show up. Then there will be more of them. Okay, I've seen enough."

"You going to run them off?"

"Not yet. Let them form up. Then we'll start their education." He smiled at Paul. "Right now I'll call for our back door team. Had to be ready on both sides of the mall." He spoke into his cell phone.

Paul stood back and raised his eyebrows. "You're back in the Marine Corps now aren't you?"

Gordon chuckled. "Oh yeah, Semper Fi!" He turned around to direct a canine team and two other officers to take up positions at empty doors.

"Two dogs?"

"Hey, if one is good, two are better." He turned to face the lot. "Okay, here's a TV truck. Let the show begin. I wonder who their leader is. He or she will be key."

"Oh, I can help there." Paul said. "I think it's Hank Polaski. He's the one they warned me about. I'll point him out. In fact," Paul squinted at the driveway and pointed. "That's him behind the wheel of the white stretch van."

"Thanks. Very helpful."

Hank pulled the van to the curb, and a stream of people exited, many with placards.

Gordon spoke into his phone. "Jerry, can you see if TV is rolling?" He looked at a guard on his far right. Jerry gave a thumbs up and nodded. Gordon faced Paul. "Okay, our turn. Paul, will you come with me and only speak if I call on you?"

Paul jerked his head around to view Gordon. "Sure, if you want. You're in charge."

"That's the idea. Let's go." He pushed open the door and strode to the street. He approached Hank. "Mr. Polaski, is this your group?"

Hank stepped close to Gordon's face. "Yes, it is. We're here to express our first amendment rights about this homophobic establishment you have here." He jabbed a finger in Paul's direction.

Gordon's lips curled up in a smile. "You haven't done your homework, sir. This is private property and you've already broken several laws." He spoke quickly again in his cell phone.

"And who's going to arrest us? You and your rent-a-cops?" Hank sneered at Gordon.

"Well, we can, but in this case we have help." He looked down the street as four patrol cars rounded the corner, lights flashing, followed by a grey school bus type vehicle, labeled 'Garfield County Corrections Department'. The windows were barred and the passenger seats were behind a sturdy barrier and gate. It pulled up next to the white van and stopped.

Hank looked around at the bus and stepped back from Gordon. His eyes squinted, and he hissed. "Okay, what laws, smart guy?"

"I might answer that if I may." A police officer said as he entered the space with Hank and Gordon.

"Be my guest George. Hank, this is Sergeant George Martin."

"First of all, you sir, are trespassing. The mall owners have the court-approved right to establish rules to regulate free speech on private property, which they've done. You haven't applied to mall management for a permit to assemble. Your signs haven't been approved in advance. You are over the assembly limit, which is three people in this mall. In a moment I will order you and your people to disperse and leave the grounds. If you fail to do so you will all be immediately arrested and transported to the county jail for arraignment. Do I make myself clear?"

Hank looked at his people, already returning to their van. "Yes, very clear. Okay, okay, we're leaving."

Paul interrupted, "Gordon, is it all right with you if I have a short personal conversation with Mr. Polaski?"

Gordon intoned, "Yeah, I guess so. May I listen in?"

"Sure." Hank, Paul, and Gordon walked a few steps away from the crowd. Paul turned to Hank. "Hank, I know you're mad at us right now so this may not be the best time to talk like reasonable men. But first, let me say I forgive you. I realize you don't like our position on some issues, and I won't debate them with you. But I also want to apologize. I didn't give you a fair hearing when you and Anton first came into The Prayer Place. I guess you know he's healed of HIV and off his meds now?" Hank nodded. "Well, the power that did that is what we are all about. If you want to learn more about it, I'd be happy to help explain how it works. Not here and now, of course, but come back and I'd love to talk about it."

Hank looked at Paul with a softened expression. The tension seemed to drain out of his body. "You know what? I just might do that. What you did for Anton was"—he appeared to search for a word—"remarkable."

"Perhaps the word you want is 'miraculous.'"

Chapter 41

Eddie and Doctor Majoros approached The Prayer Place. "Eddie, I'm not so sure this is such a good idea. I feel like I'm encroaching on someone else's territory."

Eddie came to a halt and faced his companion. "Hey, Doc. It's okay. You wanted to see what this is about. You know it's real. Look at me. With all due respect, you didn't heal me. Jesus did. Come on, check it out. It'll be fine."

The doctor smiled. "Okay, let's do it."

Eddie held the door open for him. Mary stood at the counter. "Hi Eddie. So good to see you again. You look marvelous. And you must be Doctor Majoros. Eddie called to make an appointment for you with Paul."

"Yes, he told me. Thank you for making time. I, ah, wanted to come see this miracle store for myself."

"That's great. He's almost done up with an appointment. Will you want prayer while you're here?"

"Hm. I'm not sure. I hadn't thought about that."

"Might I suggest you fill out our usual form so we can get better acquainted? If you have a prayer request in mind, jot it down. It doesn't have to be for you although we encourage people to come for themselves."

Eddie grinned. "Hey Doc, how about they pray for all your patients? Never know what might happen."

The doctor smiled. "I suppose that's true. But I have to respect patient confidentiality. I wouldn't do this without their permission."

"Oh yeah, never considered that." He turned to Mary. "Anyway, I want prayer. Kind of a final seal to chase out any little smidgen of cancer that might be hanging around in my body somewhere." He picked up a clipboard and started to fill it out.

Mary smiled. "Here's Paul. Doctor Majoros, this is Paul Shepard, our Director and the founder of The Prayer Place."

"Doctor." Paul bowed slightly as they shook hands. "We've seen Eddie several times, and now we get to meet you. That's a first for us. Mary said you wanted to see me?"

"Yes, thanks. I'm so impressed with Eddie's turnaround. Turnaround? Phooey, I'll call it like it is. His miracle. I'd like to see how you do it."

Paul smiled. "I'm glad you call it a miracle—and that you're here. We have no secret handshakes, no mystic potions or sacred rituals. But I'm getting ahead of myself. I tell you what, since Eddie wants prayer for any residual cancer, perhaps you could observe while we do that, and then ask questions. How does that sound?"

"Excellent. Sounds like a plan. Tell me what to do." He pulled a notebook and pen out of his jacket pocket.

Eddie beamed as they filed into a prayer room.

Paul explained, "Doctor, we always pray in teams of at least two people. So, this is Jaslyn Malka, my prayer partner here." They shook hands. "Doctor, first, let me ask you. Are you a Christian?"

"Yes, I've been a Baptist all my life. But my church didn't talk about healing."

Paul smiled, "No problem. We'll be happy to discuss whatever you want when we finish with Eddie. I assume, since you're here with him, that you believe in divine healing?"

The doctor raised his eyebrows. "I can't refute the evidence. Yes, I've seen that it's real."

"Great. Okay, Eddie. I'm so glad you're here again and brought your doctor."

"Oh, it was his idea, not mine."

"Is that right? Super. Eddie, let me anoint you in the name of the Father, the Son, and the Holy Ghost."

Paul and Jas continued to pray aloud for Eddie for a few minutes in English and their prayer language. Paul asked, "How are you doing?"

Eddie beamed. "Like a million bucks. I feel marvelous, really good. Thanks!"
He looked at the Doctor. "What do you think Doc?"

The doctor shook his head. "It's so simple. Is that all there is to it?"

Paul and Jas smiled. Paul explained, "Yes, it is with Eddie, since he's been here before. With new people we start with an interview. We want them to tell us why they're here, of course, and check for any background influences or interferences."

"Such as?" The doctor's pen was poised above his notebook.

"Such as inherited conditions, family influences, initiating traumas, residual feelings of bitterness or unforgiveness. Any of these can block healing. And we also listen to the Holy Spirit for words of knowledge."

"Excuse me?"

"You may recall a few scriptures that discuss the gifts of the Spirit, such as prophecy, wisdom, healing, words of knowledge. We often begin with a quiet period where we ask the Holy Spirit to come, fill the person with peace and serenity, and reveal any causes of their condition. Then we wait to hear from God. That's always the best clue for what to pray for.

The doctor looked confused. "You—you ask God and he tells you?"

The young threesome all nodded and smiled. Jas said, "Yes, often. In fact, while you and Paul were talking I've been listening in the spirit about you."

"Me?"

She blushed slightly, "Yes sir. I hope that's all right?"

"Did you hear anything—or however you put it?"

She nodded. "I did. Tell me, do you have a problem with your back?" She touched a place midway down his spine. "I'd say right about here."

"Good grief! That's amazing. Yes, yes I do, right where you touched me. I have a chronic back injury that has refused to yield to treatment. How did you do that?"

She smiled. "Well, I felt a pain in my back, and I was pretty sure it wasn't mine. I figured it must be yours. Would you like prayer for it?"

"Sure ... I guess, I mean, I'd be a fool to refuse."

Paul cleared his throat. "I'm sensing some bitterness or unforgiveness here too. Did it start as an injury, maybe something you didn't want to do?"

The doctor shook his head, stared at them with eyes wide open. "That's incredible! How could you know that? This is uncanny."

"No Doctor, it's just the Holy Spirit. You have no secrets from Him." Paul frowned. "Are you okay? Do we need to take a break here?"

"No, no. Let me explain. I worked a summer job in college and my boss told me to move a concert grand piano by myself. I had to lift it over a bunch of cables on a stage. He insisted. It wasn't on wheels and was far too heavy. I couldn't do it, and I hurt my back. I was furious. I even thought about suing him-or the University."

Paul rested his hand on the doctor's shoulder. "Can I touch you here?"

"Sure, whatever you want."

"Thanks. I sense that your anger at this incident has come back."

The doctor nodded.

"That's understandable. James 5:16 says 'Therefore confess your sins to each other and pray for each other so that you may be healed.' In this case your sin would be not forgiving your old boss for asking you to do the impossible. That sin of unforgiveness can interfere with your healing. Are you with me?

The doctor nodded.

"Okay. So, when we forgive someone, we're not saying what they did was okay. It wasn't. But we're saying we've decided not to hold it against them any longer. It's an act of our will—for us, not for them. It means we no longer allow their behavior to affect our peace of mind. We turn away from it instead.

What was your boss's name, first name only?"

"Pete."

"Can you do that for Pete?"

"Gee, I don't know. I'll try."

"Okay, I'll ask you to close your eyes and follow my words. Is that all right?"

"Sure."

Paul led the doctor in a prayer for forgiveness for Pete. Then he moved on to pray for total healing of his back injury. Jas joined in spontaneous prayer, and closed with "In Jesus name.".

They all looked at the doctor. He moved his head back and forth, then rotated his shoulders. After a moment he stood up. He swung his arms around and bent over. When he straightened up tears streamed down his cheeks. "It's gone, totally gone."

Chapter 42

Kamal stared at The Prayer Place from his kiosk. Where was Paul? What was he doing? Who did he talk to? Was he armed—he didn't think so. Was anyone armed? No way to tell. Not likely. If they had any idea what he planned, they'd be armed for sure. But how would they know? For that matter, how did they do their healing thing? Would the same power warn them? They had strange powers. He had to be careful around them.

Paul usually came and went from sight in less than a minute. He'd disappear into one of the little rooms for twenty or thirty minutes at a time.

Could Kamal catch him in one of those rooms? He wasn't ready to enter The Prayer Place to find out. Somehow he had to get close enough to Paul to put a fatal bullet in him.

His heart raced, his arms ached from tension, and his breath came is short gasps. The man was a *shayātīn*, a demon, an infidel demon. Paul must die, but he had strong powers. Not to be underestimated. What might uncle Ahmed say? "Be smart, study, plan, practice—then execute." Okay, so he studied, again. Day after day at the mall, he found no hope, no plan. Now what would Uncle Ahmed say? "Study different."

Kamal took a deep breath, let it out, and relaxed. His rage faded. His thoughts came together. He couldn't do it at the mall. Too many people, too many things beyond his control, impossible to predict. Someplace else. But where?

Kamal turned to his kiosk and sold a purse and two belts to people who came out of The Prayer Place. He tried to be nice, but closed his ears to their talk of their cures. Even as he ran their credit cards, his mind focused on Paul. Where did he live? No idea. Did he drive to work alone? Where did he eat? No idea. Be smart Kamal. Follow Paul, learn his habits outside the mall. Paul worked five or six days a week now. What did he do on Sunday?

Kamal closed his kiosk in time to sit in his car and watch the employees stream out their entrance. After a while Paul and his three college friends came out and headed for a small vehicle. He started his car and waited until they pulled out. One woman drove. Paul and his friend sat in back. At the exit of the parking lot, Kamal waited until a couple of cars passed and then pulled in behind them. If he maintained that distance and kept two or three vehicles between them he hoped they wouldn't notice. Just as long as he always kept them in sight. He shook his head. Cars changed lanes, stopped for passengers. Surveillance was not easy. If he had to do this multiple times, they might spot him. Paul knew him. The others would too. He needed a disguise, perhaps a hat, and a jacket with a big collar. In fact, if he had to do a lot of this, he'd need more than one disguise.

They pulled into a pizza place. Now what? If he walked in, they'd recognize him. He pulled into parking lot two doors down and across the street, behind an overgrown bush. Their table was right next to a window. They ordered right away. They probably ate there often and were familiar with the menu. *What am I going to do for dinner?* His stomach was growling, and he'd not thought to bring food. He spotted a chili place a few doors away. If he moved fast, he'd grab something and eat in his car. He jumped out and jogged over to try it.

Oh no. Several cars snaked out the drive thru and a line waited inside too. *Give up and go hungry, or wait it out?* His stomach rumbled, so he waited in line. The only safe order was what they claimed was all-beef chili. Their hot dogs had to have pork. At last, he ordered a Cincinnati four-way chili with beans and a Coke to go. They seemed to take forever. His thoughts turned to Paul at the pizza parlor window. If he walked up from the side they might not notice until he stood next to them. He could shoot him right through the window. *Why not? Do it tonight!*

When his food came, he snatched it up and hustled back to his car. He dropped the food in the passenger seat and reached under the his seat for the Makarov. He knew it fit in his jacket pocket because he'd tried it before. His pulse raced as he glanced around to be sure nobody saw him, he slipped it in his pocket, and walked casually toward the pizza place. *What? Where'd they go? Their table was empty. What happened?*

Did they change tables? He took a chance, pushed open the door, stepped in, and scanned the crowd. No sign of Paul and his friends. He slipped back out and hustled back to his car. On the way he realized that their car was gone too. He should have looked for that first, followed it. Not now. Too late.

After a cold, lonely meal in his car, he drove back to his apartment. Why was this so difficult? How hard would it be to walk up to Paul and shoot him? His uncle Ahmed would say, 'Study, plan, practice, then execute'. What should he do? He took a deep breath and leaked it out. He knew. Try again.

Two evenings later after work Kamal watched Paul and Caleb turn into a big white house with a long, curvy driveway. That must be Paul's house, or his parents'. No way would Kamal drive up there. But what if they just stopped to visit and lived some place else? Would they leave there in the morning? Where could he hide and wait for them? The side of the road wouldn't work. Too obvious. The gas station near their corner might do.

The first thing the next morning he pulled in next to the gas station and waited. He chose a spot out of the view of the clerk inside. But somehow the guy must have seen him because after a while he came out and rapped on Kamal's window. Kamal rolled it down.

"Hey buddy, what are you doing here? Are you going to buy something?"

"Oh, sorry. A friend's supposed to meet me here. Is that okay?"

"Yeah I guess, but don't make it a habit."

Not good, not good at all. The man would remember him, recognize him. He drummed his fingers on his steering wheel as he studied the road in his rear-view mirror. *There they are!* Paul and Caleb cruised past the station without a glance.

Okay, that's where Paul lives. Now what?

Sunday. What does he do on Sunday? Does he go anywhere? Could he loiter in the station again and follow them? The station stood alone, surrounded by houses. Was there a different clerk on Sunday?

There was, a young kid. This time Kamal asked the clerk if he might park there while he waited for a friend.

"Yeah sure, it's okay. I don't care." Right answer.

He'd been there almost an hour when an older couple rolled by in a big cream-colored, late model Lincoln Continental. They must be Paul's parents. Paul and his friend sat in the back. Kamal managed to slip in behind them and not get cut off or trapped in a red light. It wasn't easy.

After twenty minutes they pulled in a church entrance and followed the signs around back to park. Kamal hesitated but then trailed them into the lot. He drove to the back of the lot and parked facing the church. It was a boxy, cream-colored building, with air conditioning ducts on the side, and a low metal roof. 'Fresh Fire Church' was emblazoned on a sign over the double glass doors.

Paul and family walked briskly into the church. How long would they be there? He had no idea. If it was an Islamic temple, they might be there an hour—on Friday evening. But here? Sunday? No clue. He'd never attended a Christian service, never even been inside one of their churches. Could he look around? Immediately his stomach clenched, and he started to sweat. No, not today. Ahmed's voice spoke in his head again. "Study, plan, Kamal, plan. What should he do?

A wide mix of vehicles continued to fill up the parking lot. Okay, sit tight. People nearby ignored him as they hurried into the building. He'd wait until his quarry came out and follow them. He patted the gun in his jacket pocket. Sweat ran down his brow. He'd have to take off his jacket or roast. But then, where to hide the gun? Aha, problem solved. He laid the gun on the seat beside him, yanked off his jacket, and dumped it over the gun.

As he sat and waited, lively music came from the building. From time to time someone came out to smoke. He smiled at the variety of people streaming in, black, white, brown, lots of kids, even heathen girls in short skirts and some older people from The Prayer Place. They'd recognize him and want to talk. Most wore casual clothes, even jeans. Young and old. More women than men. Lots of variety. Good, he'd fit in. But he'd need a disguise. ,

After a while he got out, stretched and strolled around. No police, no guards, no cameras. Also good. He could do this. Kamal's face broke out in a grin. Shoot him in church. Yes. *Allahu Akbar*!

Chapter 43

Mary dropped a folder into the out box as she glanced out into the mall. Uh-oh, is that Vestal Hartwig? *Lord let her pass by.* No such luck. The albino witch strode along the mall, her eyes fixed on the Prayer Place." She made a beeline toward their door. Mary covered her mouth with her hand, punched a speed dial and spoke quietly into the phone. "Mall Security? This is Mary Robinson at The Prayer Place. Can you send someone down here? I think we have a situation about to develop."

"Be right there."

"Thanks Gordon. See you soon." She studied Vestal as she stomped into The Prayer Place. Even though Vestal's flattering off-white knit top, flared matching skirt, and sandals blended well with her milky white skin, an angry frown creased her forehead, her eyes flashed harshly, and she scowled through bright red lips.

Mary pasted on a smile to sound cheery. "Hi, Vestal. Are you here for prayer?"

"In your dreams, little girl," Vestal snarled as she strode into the room and planted both legs apart to glare at the visitors waiting for prayer. She pointed an accusatory finger at them. "I curse all of you people in the name of Satan! You are doomed. All doomed."

A toddler sitting on her mother's lap whimpered. The mother grabbed up her belongings and scooted out the door with the child. Another couple jumped up in alarm and prepared to leave. Vestal whirled around to glare at Mary. "See! Satan rules here. Not your puny god!" She whipped a finger in Mary's face. "Don't you move, girl!"

Mary shrank back in her chair and prayed under her breath. This was a formidable woman. What was she going to do?

Vestal pranced down the center corridor between the prayer rooms, shrieking and screaming an unintelligible song. People popped out of the prayer rooms. She looked around the break area and charged back to Mary. "Where is he? Where is that do-gooder boyfriend of yours? That Paul guy?"

Mary took a deep breath. "Paul isn't here. Jesus, Jesus, Jesus."

Vestal got right in her face and shrieked. "Silence, girl! If you want to live, you will be silent!"

Mary retreated behind her chair and snatched a clipboard against her chest. Vestal's hands were empty, no weapons, but the witch was reaching into her purse. She pulled out a small glass jar with a clear liquid in it. Acid? Acid to throw on her? Where was that security guy? "No!" Mary screamed. "Get away from me. Get out of here!" She stopped cowering and stood tall, surprised at her own authority.

Vestal stepped back with a sneering grin. "Soon, little girl, soon. My work here is almost done." She loosened the top on the jar a half turn, swung it next to her side, and lofted it down the corridor like a corn hole toss. The bottle sailed up and crashed down, shattering glass and splashing liquid all over the floor. The penetrating stench of dead fish immediately filled the entire place.

Vestal dashed out of The Prayer Place, right into Gordon Remington's firm grip. "You are under arrest, lady, for disturbing the peace and vandalism." He grabbed her wrists and snapped handcuffs on them. He yanked her away from the door as Mary and the other people streamed out of

The Prayer Place. They all reeked of dead fish. Many held their nose. A few retched and gagged.

"Yech!" Gordon said. "What is that stuff? What did you throw in there?" He looked at her red face. "You're now facing a chemical assault charge too."

Vestal's eyes filled with tears and her voice shook. "You can't put me in jail. Do you know what they do to people like me in jail? I won't last a day. I can't do it."

"You should have thought of that before you threw it. What is it?" he yelled. His grip left a red mark on her bare white arm.

"I'll tell you, but no jail. No general population. They'll destroy me." She looked at him as if she expected a reprieve. "Okay, it was DMA, dimethylamine. It's water soluble, and easy to wash off with lots of water."

Gordon looked at Mary, who confirmed. "I got it. DMA. We'll get it cleaned up. Should we get the fire department to flush it out?" she asked.

"Good idea." He responded, pressed the button on his shoulder microphone, and called for the mall fire crew. "Tell them she says it's a chemical called dimethylamine." Then he turned to Vestal. "As for you, lady. It's out of my hands where they put you. The judge will decide that. However, I'll recommend confinement until your trial. You're a definite flight risk, and a hazard to society."

As he turned again to give directions to the fire crew she screamed, "No, no!" yanked out of his grip and turned her back to him. In a practiced motion she slipped her fingers under her skirt waist, pulled out a small razor knife, slid the blade out, reached up and sliced one of her carotid arteries, then the other. Gordon grabbed for her wrist but slipped in the blood spurting out of her neck. She gave a weak shriek at him, and sliced through the veins in one wrist. She took a few steps and collapsed on her side in a pool of her blood. Mary knelt next to her in prayer. "My final sacrifice," came from Vestal's white lips in a barely audible whisper. Her head dropped, her body stilled, as she stared with sightless eyes.

Chapter 44

Gloria Sherwood, the mall manager, sat at the corner of the conference room table, nursing her second cup of coffee. The seat next to her was filled by Nelson Meier, the mall's primary owner. Although a smallish man, streaky grey brown hair, with heavy eyebrows perched above an aquiline nose, his voice rumbled when he spoke. "Gloria, as I said, when I first learned of this Prayer Place thing, I had my doubts. Major doubts. But the numbers don't lie. This has been the best summer for your mall in a long time. I considered putting this mall on the market, but no longer. In fact, some of my competitors are sniffing around to find out how we do it."

"That's just it, Nelson, we don't. It does itself. I haven't put a nickel into promotion. The only special treatment I give these folks is to be sure Gordon Remington and his security people keep them safe. They've had more than their fair share of opposition too. That albino witch committing suicide right in front of the place a couple days ago came as a total shock. We contained it as much as we could. But there's no way to keep something like that totally quiet. Thank goodness nobody got a video of it or it'd be all over the social media—and the news." She studied him. He rarely visited the mall, so she was on stage today, front and center. "What did you think of our statement for the local news last night? Did you see it?"

"Oh yeah." He arranged himself in his seat. "It was about all you could do in the situation. In fact, it was better than some might have, because you gave The Prayer Place a little promo. I hope this incident doesn't cut down their traffic."

"I hope so too." Paul opened the door for Mary. "Hi, come on in. I want you to meet Nelson Meier, my boss and the mall's owner. Nelson, this is Paul Shepard, and Mary. I'm sorry, I don't know your last name."

"Robinson, but Mary is fine."

Gloria smiled. "Nelson, as you may've heard, Paul came up with the idea for The Prayer Place, and Mary is his business manager."

Nelson smiled at them. "Impressive, very impressive." Frank Shepard peered in the door, then opened it wide. "This must be the place." He glanced around. "Hi son. Hi Mary. Hardly see you two anymore—except on television." He chuckled and reached for Nelson's hand. "Hi, I'm Frank Shepard, Paul's father and the lessee of the space they're using."

"Yes, I recognize that. We'll need to talk about it." Nelson replied. "Gloria, we're expecting two more, right? From the college?"

She smiled and pointed to the door. "Yes, and here they are. Nelson, this is Dr. Richard Schneider–Dean of Branham University, and Dr. Nancy Henning, Paul's advisor and instructor for this project." She looked at them. "Did I get that about right?"

Richard nodded.

"Good. I'm Gloria Sherwood, the mall manager, and this is Nelson Meier, the principal mall owner. Although I convened this group, and I thank you all for coming—it's Nelson's meeting. He asked me to invite all the important people associated with The Prayer Place." She paused and looked around. "Have I missed anyone?" They all shook their heads. "Good! Before we begin there's coffee, soft drinks, and

Danish on the sideboard. Help yourself." She turned to face her boss. "Nelson?"

He cleared his throat. "Thanks, Gloria. First, let me thank you all for coming. I appreciate it. As I told Gloria, I was skeptical about your little operation. Paul, I admit it. To my knowledge, this has never been done. But now, with over two months under your belt, it's obvious that, from the mall's standpoint, it's a major success. You bring people in from three states, some from hundreds of miles away. Any mall in the country would give their eye-teeth for that kind of draw. And I realize that wasn't your purpose at all."

Paul, Mary, and Frank all beamed. Paul said, "You can thank me if you want, but the real credit goes to Jesus Christ."

Nelson's face colored. "I see. Well, you're on much better terms with Him than I am. But that brings me to my reason I asked you here this afternoon. To put it in a nutshell, we don't want The Prayer Place to stop. For you this is a summer project. From our standpoint, it should continue." He studied each guest, one by one. "Normally, I'm on top of mall businesses-market share, strategies, plans, and so forth. Not this time. To be honest, I haven't a clue what it'll take to keep your doors open."

Paul squeezed Mary's hand, who wiped her eyes. "Well, sir, Mary and I, and two of our colleagues, have to return to Branham this fall to finish our degrees. So, I guess it's up to the local church to find the staff, and a new director and manager."

Dr. Schneider cleared his throat. "Possibly not. We at Branham have been discussing this same question. It's obvious that a stint here has been an incredible educational experience for our four students, one we want to offer on a continuing basis."

Nelson interrupted. "Are you saying you'd provide the staff for operations after they leave?"

Richard held up his hand. "Not so fast, sir. I was relating the outcome we'd like. Neither Dr. Henning nor I are ready to say that Branham will staff The Prayer Place. We have many things to work out, some of which have to do with money. How do we support these students? Housing, medical coverage, travel, supplies, and so forth." He stopped talking to study Nelson and Gloria. "So, my answer today to your question is a definite 'maybe'. As you may know, universities are often very slow to make changes like adding an on-going out-of-state missionary-type program to their curriculum."

Nelson frowned and pursed his lips. Then he nodded, looked up at Paul and Mary. "I see. Tell me, how many people are on your current staff?"

Paul looked at Mary. "Thirty-two."

"And who are all these people? Only four come from Branham, right?"

Paul smiled. "The rest are volunteers from my home church, Fresh Fire."

Nelson nodded. "Appropriate name it seems. But who are they? I mean, as I understand it you're open from noon until eight, six days a week."

Paul and Mary nodded.

"And how many staff do you need at one time?"

Paul raised a hand in response. "Since our traffic has increased, ideally we'd need at least eight to pray, plus Mary on the desk. If we don't have that many we cut back on the number of people we can serve. We hate to do that of course. Actually, if we had more people and more space, I'm sure we could serve more. Don't you think so, Mary?"

"For sure." She looked at Nelson. "When we began, people came in from the mall whenever they felt like it. But we've had to institute a sign-up system for appointments. That's the only fair way to handle it. If I had the time, I'd put it on a web page, but I'm way too busy. And right now we're hard pressed to handle the demand."

"And it's all free, right? No charge?" Gloria asked.

Paul and Mary shook their heads. "Oh no, we'd never charge." Paul said, as he turned to Mary,

She nodded. "Paul's right, but we had to put out a donation box because people kept asking how they could donate. Again, if I had time, I'd set up to receive credit card donations. Some people want to give more than they carry in cash."

Nelson raised his eyebrows. "Well, how much a week do you get now?"

"Two or three hundred dollars is typical. It pays for supplies and upgrades to some of our furnishings. We started with a card table, for instance."

Nelson leaned back. "This is a fabulous story." He looked at Gloria. "I'm so happy you invited me." He pursed his lips and frowned. "However, it occurs to me that we may have one person missing here. The pastor of this Fresh Fire Church. That's where the manpower is coming from."

Gloria sat up. "I think you're right. I'm so sorry."

Nelson patted the back of her hand. "That's okay. We are all here to learn. It's been a real education for me. And there're at least two more things I'd like to explore." He faced Frank.

"Mr. Shepard, this store space is yours, correct?"

"It's Frank, please. And yes, my wife expects to open a quilt shop this fall. So, when I learned this space was available, I grabbed it. It was ideal for Paul for this summer."

"Does that mean you'll want it back before long?"

"Ah, yeah. That was the plan. This is the first anyone's talked about keeping it open."

"Well sir, let me say if we can keep The Prayer Place open, would you consider another space here in the mall?"

Frank frowned. "That depends. One virtue of this space is that Marina, my wife, would have few modifications to make. That was true for Paul too. The other factor is the lease terms."

Nelson held up a hand. "Okay, these people aren't here to watch us negotiate a new space for you. However, I will commit now that your new space will not cost more than what you expected to pay for the current one."

Frank smiled, "That's very generous, but I have to ask, who'll pay the rent on The Prayer Place if I pull out?"

Nelson grinned. "I will. I want to make this work. What else can we contribute?"

"Wow!" Paul's eyes were wide open. "That's amazing." Everyone at the table nodded in agreement. Then Paul's brow wrinkled. "You said there were two more subjects you wanted to explore. What's the second one? Is it as big a bombshell as the first?"

Nelson laughed. "No. I was a skeptic and had to be shown. Well you showed me. So my question is, 'Why is it so popular? What brings people from three states here?'"

All eyes turned to Paul. "That's easy. God shows up, and people get healed. Lots of them. Not all, and we make that clear to them. But most do. Some are miraculous."

Nelson's lips tightened. "I confess I am not a Christian. I was raised Jewish but haven't practiced in years, so this 'God heals' business is all new to me. Without a long religious discussion, it occurs to me that your success depends on the people who pray, how they do it, or whatever? Am I on the right track here?"

Paul wagged his head, "Sort of. We have no magic potion, no secret incantations or rituals. But yes, if we don't have the right people pray it would all fall flat. Nothing would happen."

"So, when you consider someone new for your staff, what do you look for?"

Paul frowned and pursed his lips. "Since they all come from Fresh Fire so far, I don't worry about their theology." He stopped. "Okay, what's the most important thing about each of my staff people?"

Nelson shrugged his shoulders.

Paul smiled. "I would say that they all hear from God."

Nelson glanced at his watch. "I see." He looked up. "Actually, I don't see. Not at all." He sighed. "It's obvious I have a great deal to learn about healing. And I'm not the person to put together a proposal to continue The Prayer Place. In fact, after I listen to you all here, I'm not sure if it's possible. The secret is that it works, people get healed. I get that. But you, Paul and Mary, and the team you've attracted are unique individuals."

"Professors, I'd feel a lot more comfortable if Branham could see a way to lead and staff the effort. But you've said that's a real stretch, and there's no assurance that you'd find people like these two.

He looked at Gloria, then around the room. "So, folks, I'm sorry but I conclude that short of a miracle, it isn't going to happen."

Paul chuckled. "Well sir, we know who to go to for that."

Chapter 45

Paul, Mary, Frank, and the professors made their way back to The Prayer Place and gathered in the break area. The waiting room was packed. One lady sat next to a young child who wore huge black sunglasses. An obese woman sat in an electric scooter filling out one of Mary's clipboards.

As they sat down at the table, Dr. Henning said, "That was quite a meeting. Mr. Meier seemed disappointed." Others nodded. "He's right about one thing. If you're going to stay open, we have to do it. He can't."

Paul said, "Don't forget the local church. I believe that's the crux of staffing. Branham can't send an entire class up here for a semester, can they?"

Dr. Schneider chuckled. "Not hardly." He seemed pensive, then said, "Paul, would you like to lead us in prayer about this? Then we need to be on our way."

"Sure." They joined hands and Paul asked the Lord to bring the people He wanted to form a new Prayer Place team for the fall.

As they parted, Frank hugged Paul and whispered, "I am so proud of you I could almost explode."

"Oh no, Dad. No more excitement, please."

They both laughed. Mary whispered, "What did he say?"

Paul explained, and she joined in the merriment.

"You ready to go back to work, Mary?" She nodded as they approached Jas at the desk.

Jas stood up. "Am I glad to see you. I'd love to hear what happened in your meeting, but we're backed up here."

A few minutes later, Jas and Paul stood in a prayer room as Mary held the door open. The lady from the lobby led in the young child with the dark glasses. She handed the form to Jas. It had one word, "Desperate."

Jas's eyes filled as she handed the form to Paul.

"Hi, I'm Paul and this is Jas. We'd like to pray for you. And you are?"

"Holly, my name is Holly. And this is Roger." Holly was youngish with short, straight hair, a gray-tee shirt, undecorated, knee-length shorts, and sandals. An Alabama tee shirt and denim shorts hung on her son's slight frame beneath his large, dark glasses and brown rough-cut hair.

Paul knelt down and spoke in a low and gentle voice. "Hi, Roger." He reached out and touched Roger's hand.

Roger let go of his mother's hand and took it. "Hi," he said in a weak voice.

"You doing okay Roger?"

"Yeah, I guess."

"How old are you?"

"I'm almost nine." The boy smiled.

"Nine, that's a great age."

Paul looked at Holly. "I assume you're here for Roger." She nodded.

"What is your specific request?"

She removed Roger's glasses. "From birth. It's called anophthalmia." His eye sockets were totally empty.

Jas gasped. Paul blew out a breath and smiled. "Holly, you're in the right place. If you don't mind, I'd like to anoint him with oil, and then put my hand on his eye sockets. Is that all right?" She nodded again.

"Roger, did you understand what I asked your mother?

"Yeah, I guess. What's 'anoint' mean?"

"Good question. I'm glad you want to know. It means I put a little drop of olive oil on my finger and then touch your forehead with it. Then we'll say a little prayer. In your case I'd like to touch your eye sockets too. Is that okay?"

"Okay."

Paul let Roger sniff the oil. "This is olive oil from the Holy Land with frankincense perfume in it. There's a place in the Bible that says if you are sick or have other problems, you can ask the elders to come and anoint you with oil and pray for you, and you will be healed. Although that was written about two thousand years ago, it's still true today. That's why your mom is here. Pretty cool, eh?"

Roger smiled. "Yeah, I never heard of that."

"Many people haven't, but it's true." He anointed Roger's eye sockets, gave a brief prayer for the Holy Spirit to come, and rested his fingers on the sockets. Then he was silent for some time. Jas's lips moved in silent prayer. Paul called on the Holy Spirit and commanded functional eyes to form, over and over. He smiled and asked Jas to pray out loud too.

Paul's mouth extended into a broad grin. Minutes later, he opened his fingers to reveal two small, new brown eyes. Holly gasped. "I don't believe it! How can this be?"

Jas said, "Jesus's power in us."

Paul held his hand up to silence them. "Good. Jas, keep it up." Paul covered Roger's eyes again and continued to pray for completion of his eyes, and the optic nerves. After a few minutes he lifted his hand. "That's better."

Roger's big brown eyes with long lashes viewed the world for the first time. Roger blinked. "I can see. I can see something!"

Paul smiled again and nodded. "That's great Roger. I think we're almost done." He covered his eyes again and prayed and commanded the eye muscles and nerves to form and attach and function perfectly. Meanwhile Jas rocked and prayed under her breath. Holly covered her mouth as tears filled her eyes. This time, when Paul removed his hand Roger looked around. He touched his mother's face. "Mom, I can see you, I can see you!" He laughed hard and threw his arms around her.

Holly sagged into a chair sobbing and held her head. "It's a miracle, a genuine miracle." She turned to Paul and Jas. "Thank you so much! How can I ever repay you?"

They both shook their heads. "Oh no. God provides His mercy free, for all who ask. You came in desperation for your son. He knew that. His healing is our reward. Yes, it's a miracle."

Roger took his mother's hand. He touched the tears streaming down her cheeks. "Mom, are you okay? I can see. I can really see! I'm not blind anymore!"

She wiped her eyes and blew her nose. She shook her head and choked out, "I'm okay, honey. I'm amazed at this incredible miracle. These are tears of joy, not sadness." She kissed his forehead and hugged him. "I love you so much, so very, very much. Oh, Roger, now you can run and play with all the other kids."

"Yeah, I sure can. Can we call Dad? Can I call him?"

"Of course, dear. He won't believe it either." She hugged Paul and Jas together. "Thank you both again. Thank you so much." She grabbed Jas's arm for support as she stood up. "I'm still shaking."

Roger took her arm. "I can help you, Mom. I can see now. Come on Mom. I can help you." He led her out of the prayer room toward the exit.

***

Across the corridor, Rena eased her battery-powered scooter into the prayer room. She grunted to herself. Nobody even came close to how big she was. Her loose flowing Hawaiian-style dress hung down to her flip-flops. She touched her short, curly hair and her favorite decorative scarf, the prettiest thing about her.

"Hi, I'm Cal, and this is Loretta. You must be Rena."

"I am." Her scooter barely fit in enough to close the door. "Hi Cal, Loretta." She wiped perspiration off her forehead. "Thank you for seeing me. I've never been to anything like this, but I thought it would be worth a try."

Loretta studied Rena's form for a moment. "Rena, you've got quite a list of issues here. Why don't you tell us in your own words where we should start? What's the worst thing you deal with?"

A faint smile crossed her lips. "Okay. I guess the worst is the pain I have whenever I try to do anything. My joints ache—my knees, my hips, my legs. Even my arms and my back hurt. And breathing. It's hard to get enough air. I have to sleep in a recliner so I can sit up part way. If I lie flat I can hardly breathe."

Loretta hummed to herself. "Rena, do you have a doctor? Is there a diagnosis for any of this?"

"Oh, I have doctors for my doctors. My poor husband carts me all over town to various specialists. And it's a real struggle just to get in and out of the car."

"I'm so sorry. What do they tell you?"

Rena sighed. "Naturally they say to lose weight, but that's another story. I've tried all kinds of treatments, and nothing works. And they say I have arthritis, diabetes, congestive heart failure, and I don't remember what all. My joints are wearing out. And I'm only forty-three."

"Can I ask, 'Have you always been over weight?'"

"No. Well, I've never been what you would call skinny, but after my second baby I ballooned up. And when he died." She stopped and wiped her eyes. "After that, I ate and ate to dull the pain. I guess I still do."

"I'm so sorry. I've never lost a child, so I can only imagine how hard it must be." She glanced at Cal, who nodded. "Rena, I'll be honest, I don't know what to do to help you." She patted her arm, "But that's okay, because I know who does. Jesus has known you since before you were born. Did you know that?"

Rena shook her head.

"Yes, Rena, he has, and He wants you to be healthy and happy. He knows your pain, and He wants to take it away and to dry your tears for you. So, if it's all right with you, I'll anoint you with oil, and then Cal and I'll be silent before the Lord and let him speak to us and minister to you."

***

These people had a peace she didn't understand. They weren't fazed by her condition.

Loretta touched the back of Rena's hands and her forehead. "Rena, I anoint you in the name of the Father, the Son, and the Holy Spirit. Your job, Rena, is to listen and let the Holy Spirit come and minister to you. We do the praying and your job is to receive."

Rena wiped away more tears. Loretta and Cal prayed in low voices. She tried to make out their words, but soon relaxed as a peace and serenity flowed through her body that she hadn't experienced in a long, long time. Her eyes slid shut, her muscles relaxed until she imagined that she floated in a pool of warm water. A gentle breeze caressed her face, and her whole body. She took a quick look–no fan, only these two strangers, their heads bowed in prayer. She closed her eyes and settled back again. When she opened her eyes this time, she found Loretta and Cal studying her. She sat up. "Is there something wrong?"

Loretta grinned. "I'd say something is right. Rena, how are you doing?"

"Wow! Terrific. I haven't felt this good in years." She glanced at her belly, expecting to see it drooping between her legs. It wasn't there. "My goodness. What's happened?" She lifted one leg, then the other. No pain. She swiveled sideways on her cart seat and put her feet on the floor. Still no pain.

She leaned forward, took Loretta's hand, and stood up. She released Loretta and screamed. "Thank You, Jesus!" She raised her arms. Amazing! The big ugly flaps of fat that always hung down were missing. "It's gone, it's all gone. How did you do that?" She leaned over. "Look! There's my feet. I haven't done that in years. And I can touch my knees together." Tears streamed down her cheeks. "Loretta, How did you do that?"

Both Loretta and Cal laughed. "We didn't. The Holy Spirit did. It's Jesus's will for you. You might want to sit down for a bit."

"Oh no, I want to walk. Or run." She grinned. "Well, we'll leave running for later. Praise God I'm free of my scooter. Now I can give it so someone who really needs it. Thank you, thank you, thank you."

Loretta spoke seriously. "Rena, you've had a miracle weight loss here. That's for sure. But it isn't over. One thing we've learned about the Lord is that he wants us to do our part. You're still overweight, and I believe the rest is up to you."

Rena bit her lip. "I understand. I guess you're right."

"I think so. But besides your huge weight loss, you've got one thing now that you didn't have when you came in."

"What's that?"

"Hope."

Chapter 46

Kamal needed to develop a disguise that would let him attend Paul's church undetected. What did his uncle Ahmed say? Be smart, study, plan, practice. Then execute.

First, it had to be good up close. How to do that? How about an old man? That'd lower suspicion. So, how did old men look? Gray hair for sure. He'd need a gray wig, and a false beard. Also, something to color his eyebrows and moustache. Big tummy. He could pad his body like he had a big belly and get a cane. He tried to remember how old men walked, how they talked. They shuffled. Perhaps he should hang out in a park where they went. That's not a bad idea. Study, like Ahmed said.

He sat down at his computer and pulled up Amazon. 'Fake Beard for Adults' brought dozens of possibilities. He selected one and ordered it. Only twenty dollars plus shipping, extra for fast delivery in three days. He did the same thing for a matching shaggy grey wig. He smiled. This was going to work.

Now, what did Americans call old people? He tried to remember. Seniors. That's it! Senior citizens. Sometimes a customer at his kiosk asked for about senior discount. 'Seniors near me' in Google produced dozens of hits—apartments, dating services, medical insurance, centers, lots of things. Centers, that's it. Senior centers would be a good place to visit. He copied down some senior centers' addresses and headed to his car.

Kamal was excited by the time he returned to his apartment that evening. These old guys would be easy to copy. They favored cheap stretch pants, and shirts that hung over their belt. Easier to hide his gun. And cloth shoes with rubber soles and no laces. Where to get these? Better if used, not brand new. Many of them didn't seem to have a lot of money. A thrift store or Goodwill. Goodwill was a good idea.

Once again he found one near him and left immediately. They had a wide selection of clothing, all super cheap. He had to remember to shop for a fat man, not his sleek body. Easy enough.

Kamal returned and modeled his new outfit in front of the mirror. It took several tries to get the pillow to stuff right in his pants. His light blue shirt looked good with the gray slacks and shoes. Hey, how about a walk around the neighborhood? How would this work?

It was a warm evening, and the pillow made him sweat, but it worked fine. A couple of people even spoke to him. This was fun. He could fool them.

That evening the reality of walking into Paul's church gripped him. What do they do there? Do they take off their shoes, wash their hands, kneel on the floor? He had no idea. He couldn't go into Paul's church and not know what to do, what to expect. Who was familiar with American churches? Was Yasir? Call him–tomorrow.

"Yasir? *Salaam alaikum"* Silence. "It's Kamal."

"Kamal? *Salaam alaikum.* I didn't recognize your voice. How are you? It's been weeks, since our, ah, experiment."

"This is something else."

"Oh? Can you tell me about it?"

"Not right now. But let me ask, what do you know about American churches?"

"What? Are you converting to Christian?"

"No, no. Just tell me." Kamal was frustrated.

"Okay. I've been to an American church, twice in fact. It was with a girl I was interested in."

"Great! Can we meet?"

"Wh- What? Now?"

"Yeah. You remember that place near my office?"

"Sure. Ah, Kamal, this better be good."

Yasir was a little late as usual to the coffee shop. A quick wave from his friend and he plopped down across the table. "Hi! So what is this all about? You must tell me everything."

Kamal looked around to be sure they were not overheard, and bent over the table. He put his hand next to his mouth to keep the words close. "I want to shoot the guy that runs The Prayer Place. I've decided his church is the best place to do it."

"Allah be praised! Wow! Do you have any idea how to do this? Have you got a gun?"

"Yes, my uncle gave me one. It's untraceable. I will be in disguise so I can get up close. But I need to be familiar with what happens in a church, how they work. I don't want to stand out as a new guy, or different; nothing that'd attract attention." He took a sip of his coffee. "So, are churches different from a mosque?"

Yasir nodded. "Very different. First of all, you never take your shoes off, or wash your hands. When you go in, you sit in a chair like an auditorium. The men and women all sit together, sometimes even with their kids. I'm sure there's a lot of variety to American churches. What they do, how big they are, and so forth. But I'd guess they all have music. In the one I attended the people stood up to sing. The words appeared on screens at both sides of the stage. They had a band and singers up front, and the audience sang too."

"Oh no. Do I have to sing? I've never sung a single song in English."

"No, I don't think so. But when they stand up, you should too. The music can go on for a long time, like half an hour. I suppose longer in some places.'

"Then what?"

"Then you sit down, and people up front talk. Remember, I've only been twice. The first time a lady came up and announced something, I think about the kids program. The second time a guy welcomed everyone to the church and asked if anyone was there for the first time."

"Phew. Do I have to say something?"

"No. It's voluntary. Don't worry, they won't call on you."

"Good. What's next?"

"Next the pastor gives a talk. I heard them call it a sermon. When I was there, it was on different parts of their Holy Book. The Bible." Yasir was silent a moment. "Many people have their own. They opened them up when the talk began."

"Should I get one?"

Yasir shrugged his shoulders. "Hm. I guess it might be a good idea."

"No, no. I don't want to carry anything. I need my hands free."

"Then forget it. Not important. Okay, after the talk is over they asked for money. Guys in maroon sport coats came around and passed baskets up and down the aisles. Some people gave, some didn't. It didn't seem to matter. I didn't.

"Hey, Kamal, you really need to visit first to check out the church. As I said, there's probably a lot of variety in how they do it. You know, they might have an online webcast. The service I went to did.

"They have web pages?"

"Oh yeah. I'd guess most of them do. Google the church name and the town. I bet you find it."

Kamal grinned. "That'd be great. Sure beats going in ahead of time if I can study what they do on line."

***

Three days later Yasir sat at his usual spot in the Islamic Center sipping on a hookah. An old guy with a beard and a cane shuffled in his direction. "Hello Yasir."

"Ah, hello. Do I know you?"

"Oh very well, I'd say." The old guy's voice creaked.

He stood up. "I don't think so."

The old man grinned and said in a normal voice. "It's me. Look closely."

Yasir's eyes bulged. He grabbed the man's arms. "Kamal?"

Kamal laughed out loud. He twirled around and held up his cane like a rifle. "What do you think? Gottcha!

Chapter 47

Paul and Loretta waited on the curb at the mall's main entrance. They had dressed for the ninety degree heat, Paul in tan shorts, a dark blue "Miracles Happen" tee shirt, and Birkenstocks. Loretta's cool and comfortable filmy light green short-sleeve blouse, dark green shorts, and sandals were perfect for the day. Paul pointed. "Here he is now." A black Tahoe rolled around the corner and stopped. He reached for the front passenger door.

She motioned him to sit in front. "I think it's better if I sit in the back with Sybil, don't you?"

"Good idea." He opened her door for her. "Hi Pastor. Right on time. You doing okay?"

"Better than I deserve. You two ready for this?"

"I dunno. I hope so. It will be up to Sybil, mostly." He looked at the traffic. "Do you need me to navigate here?"

Sandy laughed. "No thanks. I put her address in my GPS. "270 North, 825 East. Wexford, Indiana. It's out in the boonies but the system found it. We've got a ways to go. Did you talk to her today? Is she ready?"

Paul nodded. "As much as can be expected. I told her we'd all be there for her. I guess if she can't talk about it, it will be up to Loretta to relate what she said. "

"Oh my, I hope not." came from the back seat. "I will if I have to, but it's her story."

Sandy turned left onto the interstate. "We'll pray together first. I've got a good feeling about this."

Forty minutes later they slowed along a two-lane gravel road. "All eyes out for number 825 on a mail box, please. It should be on the right."

"There it is!" Paul cried. They turned on a dirt track that wound around a big oak tree and stopped at a small, ramshackle clapboard house. The remaining white point was flaking off. The front windows had old fashioned pull-down shades, but no drapes or curtains. The remains of a toilet paper carton covered the upstairs dormer window. A window air conditioner hummed along at the right side.

Sybil sat ensconced in a wicker chair on the front porch, shaded by the sagging porch roof." As the SUV rolled to a stop she stood up and picked her way down the front steps with care. Her baby bump had become very pronounced. She wore a flowered dress and flip-flops. "Hi." she said with little energy.

They all exited and gathered around her. Her eyes glistened as if she was ready to cry. Loretta wrapped the former witch in her arms and held on.

Paul patted her arm and whispered in her ear. "I am so proud of you, Sybil. You are amazing."

Their eyes met. "Thanks, Paul." She pursed her lips, "Okay, let's do this. If we must."

Sandy held her door for her while the others returned to their seats. He gazed into her eyes and held out his hand, which she took. "I'm Pastor Oates, Sybil. But call me Sandy. It's a pleasure to meet you. I've never heard anything like your incredible story. You are a remarkable young lady." As she settled into her seat, he slid behind the wheel and punched up the AC. "I understand that my friend, Pastor Davies, has contacted you. How's that working out?"

"Oh Pastor, they're real nice to me. They bring me to church and helped me get on my feet with food and a few clothes—even an air conditioner! I didn't need to be skeert no more. I might even get a job soon at a restaurant."

"That's great, really wonderful. Praise God." Sandy said as he studied his GPS. "Okay, the sheriff's office is out in the country. The county seat is the tiny town of Wexford." He raised his voice. "Ladies, I talked to the sheriff, Erik Messer, and explained what we'd like to do. He was very cooperative. He did say he'd invite a colleague from the legal side, since this is such an usual case." He paused to look around the corner with care before he turned. The tall corn made it impossible to see any side traffic. "I hope that's okay. No surprises, right?"

Sybil spoke in a monotone. "Okay." Paul swung around to study her. She met his gaze, her forehead crinkled. "Are you sure I gotta do this? I mean, things are going so good lately."

Loretta put her arm around her shoulder. "Oh yes, Sweetie. This is very important. You're doing the right thing."

Paul didn't want to interrupt, but spotted the sheriff's office. He tapped Sandy's shoulder, and pointed at a low, squat block building, with steel frame crank-out windows common in the fifties. It seemed large for a small rural county. Must have housed other offices. The windows in the back were barred. Several cream and tan sheriff's department cruisers filled up the back lot.

Sandy brought his car to a gentle stop and turned so all could hear. "This is it. Before we go in, could I lead us in a prayer for the Lord's protection and guidance for all of us?" They all nodded.

He started, and Paul and Loretta joined in. After the final "Amen." they sat silent for a few moments. Then Sandy switched off the car and they all exited.

They opened the Sheriff's front door to find themselves in an open but small cage-like framework that exited in a metal detector like those at the airports. A deputy announced, "All metal in the tray at the right. Any weapons—knives, scissors, etcetera take back out to your vehicle. Then pass through the detector one at a time and sign in please."

Paul whispered to Sandy, "Is your car open? I have a Swiss Army knife." Sandy handed him the key and Paul left and returned a minute later. "Thanks."

After they'd been scanned and signed in, the Deputy said. "Have a seat. I'll tell sheriff Messer you're here." He waved them to some chairs and picked up his phone. "He's ready for you now. Follow me."

The deputy ushered them down the hall and opened the door at the end to a good-sized conference room with two people already seated. The sheriff stood to greet them. Tall and erect in his tan uniform, he had a Marlboro Man air about him. A short woman, perhaps in her early thirties, sat next to him. Her light blue summer suit, white silky blouse, and simple pearl necklace set off her brown hair, brushed back in a pony tail.

The sheriff came around to shake hands. "Welcome. I'm Sheriff Messer." He turned to his companion. "And this is APA Dawn Tucker." She reached across the table to shake hands. After introductions, they took seats opposite the Sheriff and Ms. Tucker. Sandy sat at the end, with Paul, Sybil, and Loretta lined up next to him. The Sheriff said, "Sybil, let me tell you what's going to happen here. Pastor Oates has explained the general situation to me. That's why I invited Ms. Tucker to join us, to represent the Prosecutor's office. We need to determine if a crime has been committed, and if we need to open an investigation." He glanced at Sybil. "Is that clear? Any questions?"

"I understand. But what's an APA?"

Dawn smiled. "Oh, I'm sorry, we use so much jargon. It's Assistant Prosecuting Attorney. Mitchell County is too small to have its own full-time Prosecuting Attorney, so several counties formed a district that share the Prosecutor's office and Judgeship.

Sybil whispered to Loretta, who said, "Ah, Sybil asked if we might pray for God's will before we begin." She looked around at nodding heads.

The Sheriff announced. "Sure would. We should do it every time." He looked around and settled his gaze on Pastor Oates.

Sandy responded with a short prayer thanking the Sheriff for letting them pray and asking for God's guidance in the decisions they had to make, and that their hearts be open to His will for Sybil.

"Thanks, Pastor," the Sheriff said as he centered a tape recorder on the table and flicked it on. "Okay, Sybil, as I understand it, you had a baby several years ago that you gave up to the witches' group. It died a few days later in some kind of ceremony they had. Is that about it?"

She nodded.

"Okay, I realize this is very hard for you, and we'll be as gentle as we can. We appreciate your willingness to come forward.

"So, can you tell us what happened, in your own words? Why don't you start with the later stages of your pregnancy, the baby's birth, how and why you gave it up, and what happened to it up to its eventual death?"

She nodded again.

He held up a finger. "We may ask a few questions as you go, but we'll try to hold them to the end. We'll also take individual notes."

Sybil cleared her throat. "I didn't want to get pregnant. But I was high most of the time in those days and didn't know what I was doing. And I didn't know nothing about babies. I was raised in foster homes and reform schools you see." She continued for twenty minutes and repeated what she had told Paul and Loretta.

Her consistency amazed Paul.

When she stopped, they sat silent. Dawn dabbed at her eyes with a tissue, then looked at Sybil. "Sybil, first, thank you for your candor. I believe every word you said. Trust me, that's very unusual in my business. But I have a few questions. Okay?"

Sybil nodded.

"Good, first, is there any chance that the baby's remains are still around?"

Sybil shook her head. "No, like I said, the fire was real big and burned for a long time. By the time we went home there was nothing but ashes. And that was years ago. Now? Naw, there won't be nothing."

"I was afraid of that. And I guess there was no birth certificate, no record of the birth?"

Again she shook her head. "Not unless Vonnie done it—which don't make no sense. Why would she? She already knew what they was gonna to do."

"Uh-huh. And can you say who actually placed the box with the baby on the wood pile?"

She shrugged her shoulders. "I think it was Vonnie, but I ain't sure. I was awful high that night."

"But it wasn't you?"

Sybil backed up from the table. "No way. Even stoned I wasn't doin' that."

"Okay, okay. I don't mean to upset you. Do you know where Vonnie is now? How I might get hold of her?"

"Oh, I dunno." She shook her head. "Since I left the coven, they all dropped me. She might still be around. But she ain't gonna tell you 'bout what the coven does."

Dawn nodded. "Probably not." She turned to the Sheriff. "That's all I have. You have any questions, Erik?"

He nodded. "Yes, one, but first let me add to Ms. Tucker's appreciation for your honesty, Sybil. My question is, 'who lit the fire?'"

Sybil frowned and pursed her lips. "I think it was kinda everyone. A lot of the girls had candles. As I remember they threw them on the pile. They must'a put some gas or something on the wood 'cause it started to burn real quick."

"Did you have a candle?"

"Nope."

"Thank you, Sybil." He switched off the recorder and sat back a moment. "Okay, you folks can go back to Ohio. Ms. Tucker and I will confer and decide what to do next. Pastor, do we communicate through you?"

"That'd be fine." Sandy stood up, followed by the rest of the visitors. Loretta and Paul gave Sybil a big hug, and they filed out of the conference room.

***

Eric looked at Dawn. "Wow. I sure didn't know what to expect, but it wasn't that."

Dawn nodded. "That girl was totally believable. Even an all-male jury of confirmed misogynists would be moved. One female on the jury and there's no conviction. Slam dunk for the defense."

"So, Ms. APA, was there a baby?" He answered his own question. "Yes, must have been. But zero tangible evidence of it."

She nodded again.

"Was the baby incinerated? Again, must have been. But again, not a shred of forensic evidence. And who, exactly, did it?"

She said, "I give. Who?"

"A bunch of nameless witch women on a farm someplace. The one thing I'd say for sure is that Sybil didn't kill her."

Dawn asked, "So do we say 'insufficient evidence of a crime?'"

He shook his head. "I can't do that. That's your call."

She sighed. "Okay. I'll take this to the PA. He's got to play the whole tape. Then he'll earn his big bucks and tell us what to do."

"What do you think he'll say?"

"Oh, I can't say how he'll put it. His politician hat will salivate at the "Witches Burn Baby Trial" headlines in his head. But his attorney hat will say. "Don't be stupid, Brad. You'll never win.""

Chapter 48

"Mr. Shepard? This is Norma Fallon, Channel Eight News. Do you have a minute?" Her voice chimed through the speakerphone.

Paul looked at Mary, who grinned at him. "Yes," he said slowly, "what can I do for you?"

"You're a busy man. I'll come right to the point. We've heard some remarkable stories about The Prayer Place. We'd like to come out with a camera team and do a feature on it. Would that be all right?"

"Ah, when do you want to do this?"

"How about tomorrow morning? That'd give us time to edit our tapes and put it on the six o'clock news." She stopped.

Was she waiting for him to respond? It was her nickel.

"Paul, I'm sure the public will be very interested. For instance, is it true that you prayed for a young boy who had no eyeballs, and he grew some? Right there at your place in the mall?"

"Yes, that happened two days ago." Paul frowned. "Ms. Fallon, is it?"

"Yes."

"I hesitate here because we have an ethical responsibility to protect the privacy of our guests. That's what we call the people who come in for prayer. We don't open until noon, but why don't you come at, say, ten. We can tell you who we are, what happens here without violating the guests' privacy."

"Oh, I see. I had hoped we might film an actual prayer session."

Paul shook his head. "No, not without previous permission of everyone involved. We are not a circus act or stage performers." He noticed Mary's frown. "Ms. Fallon, forgive me. That was out-of-line. So, can we see you at ten? If you like you can film the facility. We can talk about how we pray for people, plus any specific cases you may be familiar with. Is that okay?"

"We can go with that. See you in the morning."

***

The next morning Paul and Mary came to work early to put things in order. Mary called Gloria Sherwood, the mall manager, to tell her their plan. Gloria thanked them for the heads up and said she'd have to call in extra security since a TV crew would attract attention.

An average height woman in a light blue blouse with a Channel 8 vest, dark blue slacks, and white tennis shoes walked down the mall with a TV crew. She extended her hand. "Paul? I'm Norma. Thank you for letting us do this. We'll try to be mindful of your time. You open at noon, correct?" Her heavy make-up was probably to look good on-camera. It blended well with her professionally styled short blond hair and wide-set blue-gray eyes.

"Yes, although I don't have to work then. Mary won't schedule me with a guest until you folks finish."

"Hey that's great. So, give me an idea of what happens here, and then we'll have you take the camera in a tour."

"Sure." He explained their appointment and sign-in system, the number of prayer rooms, and the usual length of a session. Afterward, Paul said, "I've considered about your desire to talk to actual guests who've been healed. I'm sure one lady who had a club-foot straightened, Dolly at the cookie store, would be happy to talk to you. She's at work today. And I guess somehow you're aware of Roger's new eyes?"

"Yes, that's a definite one. And the lady who lost so much weight."

"Oh, Rena. She actually called yesterday and said she'd lost two hundred pounds. In fact, she said she planned to clothes shop here today, and would like to stop in. She'd probably talk to you too."

He frowned, then asked. "Norma, I have to ask how you know so much about these specific healings. I mean they're only two days old."

Norma blushed. "My mother is Wendy Hartman, on your staff. She's so excited about all the people healed here that I can hardly shut her up."

"Then why don't you interview her? I'll caution her to not mention specific guests' names, as I confess I just did. But it's fine to talk about the healings."

"My mother? I'm supposed to report the news, not be part of it."

"Well, it's wouldn't be you in the news, it's your mother. I don't know Wendy well, but I bet she'd do a great job." He looked at Mary, who had watched their conversation. "Is she on the schedule today?"

Mary checked her computer. "Only this evening, six o'clock."

Norma seemed a little unsettled. "Huh, I'm not sure, I never considered it. She'd probably be okay, actually pretty good. She sure is all excited."

Norma looked at Paul and Mary. "You know who I'd dearly love to interview is the little boy who got the eyeballs. Is there any way to get him and his mother to talk to us?"

Again Mary turned to her computer. "Here's her sign-in form. She has a local address, in fact, close to here, and a phone number." She looked at Paul. "Okay if I call her and ask?"

"If she agrees, sure. She's already told everyone around here about it."

The clock crawled on and they went on camera. Norma interviewed Paul plus an occasional question for Mary. Norma honored Paul's insistence that they stop before guests came in. However, she could talk to guests out in the mall if they agreed.

When Rena arrived shortly after noon, Mary asked if she'd like to tell her story on TV. Rena's face lit up. "Would I?" She all but raced out into the mall.

As the TV crew was about wrap up Holly and Roger came down the mall. Norma intercepted them and signaled the crew to keep filming. When she introduced herself, Roger jumped up and down. "That's so cool! I used to listen to you on the six o'clock news. Now I can see you!"

Norma came into The Prayer Place about two. "Paul, we've got to scoot back to the studio and edit this raw footage into our feature story. I hope you get a chance to watch it. I'd love to get your impressions."

Paul took her hand, "Thanks Norma, it's been my pleasure. As I'm sure you could tell, I was skeptical at first, but now I'm sure it'll be fine. I'll still be here at work then, but I'll record it at home."

***

The next morning the line for The Prayer Place gathered as soon as the mall opened at ten a.m. Gordon Remington, mall security director, brought in ropes and stands to turn the mob crowding at the door into an orderly line. He also enabled traffic to walk past and get access to the nearby stores. An extraordinary number of overweight people, plus walkers, wheel chairs, and the blind had managed to get there.

He called his boss. "Gloria, you best get down here. That TV news story last night on The Prayer Place was the best free advertisement I've ever seen. I don't know a lot about how this place operates, but I bet they have all the people they can handle all day already right here and waiting to get in."

"Okay, on my way."

A few minutes later, she approached Gordon at a fast walk. "Wow! You were right about the crowd. How many people have got here?"

"At least a couple hundred."

"And how many a day can they pray for?"

"No clue. I'll call Paul and get him in here. We don't want these people to stand here all day with no hope of service. They'll get mad at us, not the prayer people."

Gordon punched Paul's speed dial number. "Mr. Shepard, Gordon Remington at the mall."

"Hi Gordon, what's up?"

"Your news story last night has generated a huge response. How many people can you pray for in a day?"

"Hm, let me see. Eight hours open, four prayer rooms, half an hour per person on average. That's sixty-four, max."

"Oh-oh. We've got a major problem. You better get in here pronto."

Chapter 49

Kamal checked his appearance in the mirror one last time and smirked, very satisfied. This would work. He'd practiced his old man disguise, walk, and speech for days. Nobody even detected him. A neighbor even asked if his grandfather visited him after he'd seen Kamal shuffle out to his car in disguise.

He slapped a fresh magazine into his gun, racked a shell into the chamber, and confirmed the safety switch was on. He loved how it felt in his hand. Yes, he could have spent more time at the target range, but he relied on his uncle's advice. "Get close."

This was it. Allah be praised.

Twenty minutes later he eased his car into a space behind the church and surveyed the lot. Although several dozen cars dotted the lot, it was far from full. After many hours spent studying their web-stream, he concluded that a seat on the center aisle would be best. He'd arrive not too early, about ten minutes before the start of worship. This church filled up after the official start time, which suited Kamal. He first adjusted his gun butt beneath his shirt to insure it didn't protrude. A quick glance at his watch confirmed—perfect time to go. He slid out of the car and ambled behind a family of five kids as they made their way into the church. They looked to be from India. He tried to act like a grandparent. As the gaggle entered the door, he tagged along at the rear, smiled at the greeter, but remained mute.

Inside he found the ideal seat, the fourth row on the left side of the center aisle. His gun hand was free. As he took his seat he scanned his surroundings. An older woman and a young girl sat at the other end of his row. Probably the granddaughter. Kamal caught himself chanting a Muslim prayer as he waited. *Be smart, Kamal, smart and patient. Your time for glory is near. Let it come to you.* He lowered his head as if in prayer

Although he stood when most of the audience did, he didn't sing along, even though they projected the words on the screen. *Did he see Paul in a front-row seat on the far right, next to Mary? Not sure.* Kamal wrung his hands and fidgeted in his seat. *Would this music never end?* Near the end, several women paraded around with a variety of colorful banners they got from a rack in the corner. Utterly shameful, the way they strutted and danced and showed their bodies. *Someone should shoot them.*

At last, a man came up to the clear plastic pulpit. "People, join me in this last song, and come to the front if you want prayer."

Kamal's cue. His feet slid beneath, him, ready to rise. The man took the microphone again. "Today, people, we have a special treat. Many of you know Paul Shepard. He and his friends opened The Prayer Place at the Colony Mall for the summer. Many Fresh Fire folks volunteered to join his staff. And, if you saw Channel Eight news earlier this week, you know what an outstanding success it is, and the miraculous healings that have happened again and again. Even before that program, I had asked Paul if he'd speak to us before he returns to school in a couple of weeks. So, I'm happy to say, he agreed. Ladies and gentlemen, I give you Paul Shepard! Paul, come on up here."

The audience stood, clapped and cheered. Kamal stood too. His heart raced. Sweat formed on his lip, under his arms.

He stepped out in the aisle and moved toward the podium. Paul strode over from his seat. He looked back at Mary, hopped onto the stage, and gave the pastor a hug. He looked relaxed and comfortable behind the pulpit. With the microphone up to his lips, he smiled, gazed at the crowd, but remained silent with his hand up.

Kamal took two broad steps to right in front of the pulpit. In one smooth motion he read his feet with his left foot forward, pulled out the gun, flipped off the safety, and held it in a two-hand grip. He lined up the sights on Paul's chest, shouted, "Allahu Akbar!" and squeezed the trigger. BANG! Paul staggered and grabbed the pulpit. Kamal fired again, BANG! Paul collapsed on the stage. Blood spurted from his chest.

As Kamal steadied his weapon for a head shot, a giant weight slammed him to the floor. He flared out his hands to catch himself. The gun slid out of his grip to the foot of the stage. Two huge hands gripped his wrists. The weight was so heavy his lungs could barely inhale. A deep voice spoke in his ear, "You move, and I'll tear your head off!"

***

Mary screamed and leapt to Paul's side. "Oh Paul! Paul!" She reached over to the basket of prayer cloths the deacons kept at the foot of the pulpit, scooped up and a handful, and pressed them hard on the hole in Paul's chest. The blood spurt stopped. More came out from a wound in his shoulder, and from somewhere underneath his back. "Call 911!" She screamed through the rising noise in the sanctuary. "Call 911!" She pressed the last of the prayer cloths to his shoulder wound. She shook and sobbed as she pressed desperately on his bloody chest.

George Alderman, the head of security, leaned over. "They're on the way, Mary. Keep up the pressure. You're doing the right thing."

She looked up, surprised to see two of the ushers pointing handguns at the man pinned on the floor. What was this world coming to?

Her tears blended with the blood on Paul's shirt.

Patty Weisman knelt down next to her. "Mary, let me do that. I'm an ER nurse." She yelled, "Clear off this equipment, get the pulpit out of the way! We need to stretch him out—raise his legs. And make room for the Life Squad gurney."

Patty held up a handful of fresh towels. "Okay, Mary, on three you release and take your cloths off. I'll resume pressure." She studied Mary. "One, two, three." As Mary lifted her hands and slid back from Paul's body, Patty pressed the fresh towels over the wounds.

Mary crawled a distance from Paul, eased off the edge of the stage, and slumped down in racking sobs. "O Jesus, Jesus, Jesus. Save him, save him, save him." Several soft hands touched her shoulders and back. She raised her head. Three women bent over her, eyes wet with tears.

Multiple sirens shrieked close to the building. Two police officers burst into the room, guns drawn. They found Brock Tibbs' three hundred plus pounds pinning the shooter to the floor. Within moments they'd retrieved his gun. Brock eased off, and they cuffed him and sat him up. An off-duty officer on the church security team verified he was the only shooter. One officer keyed his shoulder microphone. "Scene is secure."

Seconds later an EMT crew slid a gurney next to Paul and opened their equipment boxes. A technician put a stethoscope on Paul's chest. He listened and turned to his partner. "Air Care on the way?" His partner nodded. The lead man returned his attention to Paul. "He's bleeding out. We'll treat him here. Lose the gurney. I don't want an extra transfer to ours. Air Care has their own."

Mary looked at Paul, deathly pale, motionless. The EMTs hovered around him and started an IV. They cut away his shirt and applied bandages. A second EMT team showed up along with additional police officers. She glanced over at the shooter. His wig lay on the floor and someone must have ripped off his false beard and moustache. "Kamal?"

An officer came over. "You know this man?"

She nodded. "He's Kamal. He runs the leather goods shop in front of The Prayer Place. I don't know his last name."

The officer squatted next to her with a pad a pen poised. "Can I have your name and number? And could you come down to the station to make a statement?

Mary nodded and turned back to Paul. An oxygen mask covered his face now. They started CPR and a heart monitor. It showed an irregular pulse. The EMT said, "Need the defibrillator." A second man had it ready. They cleaned a space on Paul's chest, applied the paddles, and charged. Paul's body bucked. The trace showed a weak rhythm, very fast.

Although the oxygen and CPR continued, the trace wiggled erratically. They tried the paddles again. The trace flat lined. After four more tries the lead EMT sat back. "No pulse. Continue CPR. I'll call the doc." Moments later he explained Paul's symptoms. "Okay, doctor. Hang on. I'll shock him one more time, just to be sure." He nodded to his partner to apply the paddles and crank up the voltage. "Nothing Doc, flat line. Yeah, I agree." He shook his head to his partner and said, "That's it. No pulse, thirty minutes of CPR. I'm calling it." Glanced at his watch. "Eleven twenty-two."

Mary's eyes opened wide. "No!" she screamed. The EMTs looked around, surprised. They started packing up their equipment. "No, no you don't!" She leaped onto the stage, shoved the EMT out of the way, and kissed Paul's lips, already turned blue. Then pounding on Paul's chest, she screamed, "Paul Shepard, you get back in here! You can't leave us yet. We're not done here. I know you're out there. You get back in here right now!" She sat back and sobbed.

Paul opened his eyes. He coughed and reached for her.

Chapter 50

Paul's mind meandered through the dreams, drugs, and exhaustion cobwebs in his semi-consciousness. His eyes slid open a crack. *Hm, a hospital ceiling? How about that?* Had to be. The special lights overhead, the drapes, and assorted tubes and cables coming from the wall—probably going into him. He looked to his left and smiled. Mary sat next to him, dozing in her chair. She looked uncomfortable. Across the way, mom and dad whispered together.

He wanted to feel his body. Pain shot through his right arm when he tried to move it. They'd strapped it in a sling too.

He tried his left. Free and no pain. His fingertips traversed under the sheet to his chest. It was encased in bandages. Wires or tubes came out the side. And they'd immobilized his right shoulder in some kind of restraint. A cast?

"Oh yeah," he mumbled to himself, "somebody shot me." His dream world faded fast. *No, no, I don't want to leave it. It's so peaceful, so surreal.* But the pain of the real world crowded in.

Mary stirred and peered at him with groggy eyes. They popped wide open. "Paul! Paul, you're awake!" She reached over to hug him but stopped herself. Instead, she leaned over and kissed him. He held her head to his with his left hand.

"Now that's the way to wake a fella' up." He smiled and a wave of dizziness took over. "Hi, how are you doing?"

"Me? I'm fine. The question is 'How are you?'"

"I ache." He waved over his chest. "All over here."

His parents scrambled over next to the bed and stood opposite Mary. His mother eyes streamed tears down her cheeks. "Mom, what's wrong?"

"Oh Paul, we've been so worried. First, when you were shot. Then they said you were dead. Praise God Mary called you back."

Paul held up his hand. "Yeah, I remember now." He paused. "The ceiling, I was up by the ceiling. I saw it all—almost like a movie. The medics worked on me and then they stopped. I felt a comforting presence next to me. An angel? Then Mary demanded that I return to my body." He looked at her and reached for her hand. "I didn't want to. I hurt so much and it was so hard." He gazed in her eyes as they filled with tears. "But you said we weren't done here, that I couldn't leave yet."

Both his parents wiped their eyes. He smiled. "And you know, Mary is always right."

He chuckled but winced in pain. "No jokes folks. Hurts too much to laugh now." He slowly inhaled then relaxed. "So I came back into my body, and it hurt, it hurt a lot. It still hurts. I was so weak, and what a mess. Blood everywhere." He looked at them. "Did you see how amazed that medic was? He didn't believe it. But he did his thing, called the helicopter back."

Paul closed his eyes and mouth for a couple minutes. When he opened them again, everyone seemed to relax. "Hey people, chill. I'm not leaving here. I tried that—didn't work out. Anyway, that was the first time I ever rode in a helicopter, and I couldn't even see out the window? Bummer."

Frank said, "Son, if you want a helicopter ride, you get well, and we'll hire one to fly you around the city."

A nurse popped in the door. "How long has he been awake?"

"Oh, a few minutes. We've been chatting." Mary said, "Is that okay?"

"No, I'm sorry, it's not. This man needs total rest. He's only a few hours out of open heart surgery, and a gunshot repair. You people will have to leave—now. You can wait in the ICU waiting room. The doctor will be out to explain Paul's condition and what to expect for the next few days."

Paul watched this little speech with interest and stuck out his tongue when the nurse wasn't looking. "When are you going to tell *me* what to expect?" He noted her frown. "Okay, okay. I get it, shut up and rest. I am pretty tired, and all I do is lie around here." He tried to roll over on his side but gave up. Too painful. "I need a nap here. Tell me later." He closed his eyes and drifted off.

***

A white-coated female doctor approached the group. Close to six feet, she wore her brown hair cropped short, with the trade-mark stethoscope hung around her neck. "Family of Paul Shepard?"

Frank looked in her soft, gray eyes. "Yes, doctor. I'm Frank Shepard, Paul's father. This is Marina, his mother, and Mary, his girlfriend."

"Oh, yes, I heard about you, Mary. I'm Doctor LeCroix, Paul's heart surgeon." She looked at Mary. "Your story is remarkable. Hard to believe."

"Oh it's true. It all happened right in front of us." Marina said.

Frank nodded. "What can you tell us about Paul?"

"Well, as you know, he was shot twice at close range. The first shot nicked the top of his heart, hit a rib and deflected into his right kidney."

"Oh dear Lord!" Frank said.

The doctor continued, "Yes, it was very serious. The second shot went through the right shoulder, a clean in and out. It did a good bit of damage of course. But the first shot might easily have been fatal. Someone must have acted real fast to staunch the blood flow.

Frank and Marina both looked at Mary. The doctor did too. "Was that you?"

She nodded, unable to speak through her tears.

"Amazing," the doctor said. "In fact, everything about this case has been amazing. I'll write it up for a journal article. Anyway, when Air Care brought him in he was very weak, almost no blood pressure, very shallow respiration. We stabilized him, started a transfusion, and got him into surgery. Fortunately, I was able to repair the wound to the heart on the first attempt and then dig out the bullet. The kidney seems to function perfectly. We were afraid we might have to go in through the back to get it, but luck was with us."

"Or God." Frank suggested. "There was a great deal of prayer then for Paul."

"Well, I'm not much of a churchy person, but I have to admit you people could be right about this. Anyway, after we closed him up, Doctor Orenstein repaired his shoulder. He's an excellent orthopedic surgeon who happened to be on call. That, too, was uneventful." She stopped and looked at them. "You folks look worn out. How long have you been here?"

"Since he came in yesterday, Mary said.

"Oh my. Yes, you're exhausted. Okay, really quick, Paul will be here in ICU for the next few days while we monitor his vitals and make sure there's no infection. He'll be in quite a bit of discomfort, which we will control but cannot eliminate one hundred percent. We will not send him home as a pain med addict. Frankly, I'm amazed he doesn't show more signs of discomfort. But, be that as it may, you folks go home now, get some sleep. Hydrate, hydrate, hydrate, and eat well. All visitors are stopped as of now. I will allow one visitor this evening for twenty minutes." She looked at them and saw the parents looking at Mary. "Mary, would you like to be that one?"

"Oh, yes please! Thank you so much." She turned to Frank and Marina, "And thank you too." They all hugged.

* * *

Mary tiptoed into the room and glanced at the clock. Seven twenty. Paul lay still, a pause between each breath. He looked relaxed, with even a slight smile. "Praise the Lord," Mary whispered.

"And pass the ammunition," Paul whispered back. He opened his eyes and grinned. "Hi, beautiful."

Mary laughed out loud. "Oh you! You're supposed to be suffering, in pain, and all drugged up. Not making jokes."

"Hey, I can't laugh. It hurts too much. But you look like you need some cheering up." He reached over and took her hand. "Mary, I'm going to be okay. It'll take a while, but I'm on the mend."

"Oh, Paul." She came around the other side of the bed to give him a half hug. "I was so worried. We all were. I've no idea how many people are praying for you, dozens, or more. It's gone viral on social media. In fact, it's on TV too. Our webcast caught the whole thing, and somebody at church did a video and sent it in. It starts right after Kamal shot you. Really dramatic."

"Kamal shot me? From the leather goods place?" She nodded. "Can you get a message to him from me?"

"I dunno. I guess. He's in jail. He's lucky he didn't get shot. The church security team had guns on him within seconds." She studied Paul. "Why? What do you want me to tell him?"

"That I forgive him."

She sobbed and shook her head. "Oh, Paul. I can't do that. I haven't forgiven him. I hate him now. He's a terrorist. He's evil. Didn't you hear him yell 'Allahu Akbar' just before he shot you?"

Paul frowned. "I don't think so. It stunned me. But, it didn't look like him. The guy was a lot older."

"He wore a disguise. He planned the whole thing. Paul, he wanted to kill you."

"Doesn't matter. Scripture tells us to pray for our enemies and forgive them, so we may also be forgiven."

She squeezed his good arm. "You are a truly, truly good man, Paul Shepard. Okay, I'll try to get him the message."

"Thanks, beautiful." He closed his eyes for a few moments to rest, then smiled at her again. "So, what's happening at The Prayer Place?"

She grinned, "As you would say, dear, 'not to worry'. A great deal is happening. We're swamped with clients, and more people ask to volunteer.   We get letters asking if they can join—like from Pennsylvania, California even. Anyway, I'll get permission for more visitors tomorrow to bring you up to date."

"That's great. You know, this 'rest' thing could be habit-forming? If you don't mind, my sweet, I'd like a little goodnight kiss, and then I need to nap again."

She leaned over, and at the moment their lips met the nurse came in. "Now, people, the patient is supposed to rest here, not fall for the first pretty girl who happens by."

Paul shook his head. His eyes locked with Mary. He squeezed her hand and whispered, "You know I love you."

She nodded and smiled.

"I…I have for the longest time," he said softly.

***

The next morning Mary, Frank, Marina, and Pastor Oates filed into the room. Paul sat up straighter. "Wow! You guys have to sneak past nurse Ratchet?"

Pastor Oates handed him a stack of get-well cards. Marina put two vases of flowers on his side table, and Mary propped three stuffed bears around his bed. Paul said, "What, no TV crew?"

They all scooted their chairs next to the bed. Frank laughed. "Well, it wasn't for lack of trying. They hang around to interview us and badger the hospital to talk to you. But that lady doctor of yours is a real momma bear. Nobody gets near her cub. We had to promise to be quick and quiet."

Paul grinned and pushed the control to raise his bed to see them better. "Please, tell me you're here to update me on The Prayer Place."

Pastor Oates nodded and cleared his throat. "In part. Okay, as chairman of The Prayer Place executive committee ..."

"The what? I only got shot two days ago. Has the revolution already begun?"

They all laughed. Frank said, "Sorry, son. I'd say the revolution is over." He looked at the Pastor. "Sandy, you should be the one to tell him."

Sandy cleared his throat. "Paul, as you know, nobody wants The Prayer Place to close when you go back to school, not the church, not the University, not the mall manager and owner, and certainly not us. So, we've talked and prayed about what to do about it. And I think we've heard from God. I'm going to take a sabbatical from Fresh Fire Church to manage The Prayer Place full-time."

"Wow!" Paul exclaimed. "That's fabulous. Thank you so much. Sorry to hand it to you this way."

"No problem. It largely runs itself now with the current staff and Mary's guiding hand. In fact, my first job is to replace her, so she can go back to school."

"That's not all," Paul said, with a broad smile.

All eyeballs widened and turned to him. Marina said, "What do you mean?"

Paul looked at Mary and reached for her hand.

"Mary, my love, will you marry me?"

The End

If you want prayer for healing

Some readers may be moved to get some healing prayer for themselves or a loved one, but not know where to go. The answers these days is the Internet. Some churches have healing prayer as part of their Sunday services, and may come up on an internet search.

However I believe in general the place to start is the International Association of Healing Rooms, IAHR. They list approximately 3000 healing rooms in 72 countries. Their main website is www.healingrooms.com

The page to begin to find a local Healing Rooms is https://healingrooms.com/index.php?src=location   From there you click on the map or type in your location to search the site.

All things are possible with God.

Acknowledgements

I would like to thank the following people who contributed specific knowledge and/or encouragement and enthusiasm for The Prayer Place.

Peggy Rattray – My wonderful wife who proofread and commented on every chapter, as well as encouraged and motivated me to keep going.

Bob and Carla Fritz – Co-directors of the Healing Rooms North Cincinnati,

Pastor Randy Rice – Pastor of Life Church Westchester, Westchester, OH

Pastor/Chaplin Jody Burgin for your interest, enthusiasm, and suggestions throughout.

Middletown Area Christian Writers – Donna, Norma, Helen, Bonnie, JuneEllen, Linore, Judy, and others who challenged me to improve my plot as well as helping with the writing.

American Christian Fiction Writers Critiquers – Too numerous to name. You know who you are. Because of you I am a better writer.

The Turtle Creek Township, Warren County, Ohio, Life Squad.

Frank Courtney, Dr. Jeff Middledorf, Heather Rattray, Vincent Simmons, and Judy Woltmann.

Thank you all.

Bibliography

Copeland, Kenneth. *John G. Lake: His Life, His Sermons, His Boldness of Faith.* Tulsa, Oklahoma, Harrison House, 1995

Hagin, Kenneth E. *The Believer's Authority,* Second Edition. Tulsa: Rhema Bible Church, , 1986

Hinn, Benny. *Kathryn Kuhlman.* Nashville, Tennessee. Thomas Nelson. 1998

Johnson, Bill and Clark, Randy. *The Essential Guide to Healing.* Bloomington, Minn.: Chosen Books, 2011

Liardon, Roberts. *God's Generals.* Sarasota, Florida. Whitaker House, 1996

Pierce, Cal. *Preparing The Way,* Hagerstown, MD., McDougal Publishing, 2001

Saleem, Kamal. *The Blood of the Lambs.* New York: Howard Books, 2009

Wigglesworth, Smith. *The Anointing of His Spirit.* Edited by Wayne Warner, Ann Arbor, Michigan, 1994

28276550R00130

Made in the USA
Columbia, SC
09 October 2018